Soldiers Cry by Night

Los soldados lloran de noche

Soldiers Cry by Night

Los soldados lloran de noche

by

Ana María Matute

translated by

Robert Nugent and
María José de la Cámara

Latin American Literary Review Press
Series: Discoveries
Pittsburgh, Pennsylvania
1995

The Latin American Literary Review Press publishes Spanish language creative writing under the series title *Discoveries*, and critical works under the series title *Explorations*.

Library of Congress Cataloging-in-Publication Data

Matute, Ana María, 1926-
 [Soldados lloran de noche. English]
 Soldiers cry by night / Ana María Matute ; translated by María de la Cámara and Robert Nugent.
   p. cm.
 The 2nd novel in the trilogy which includes The merchants (1st) and The pitfall (3rd).
 ISBN 0-935480-67-6 (alk. paper)
 I. Cámara, Mária de la. II. Nugent, Robert. III. Title.
PQ6623.A89S613 1995
863'.64--dc20   94-25087
                                                             CIP
Cover photograph: Archive of the Crown of Aragon, Barcelona, Spain. From *España Colombina*, courtesy of Lunwerg and Quinto Centenario Publishers.
Cover graphics and book design by Michelle Rozzi.

The paper used in this publication meets the minimum requirements of the American National Standard for Permanence of Paper for Printed Library Materials Z39.48-1984. ∞

Soldiers Cry by Night may be ordered directly from the publisher:

          Latin American Literary Review Press
          121 Edgewood Avenue
          Pittsburgh, PA 15218
          Tel (412) 371-9023 • Fax (412) 371-9025

ACKNOWLEDGMENTS

This project is supported in part by grants from the National Endowment for the Arts in Washington, D.C., a federal agency, and the Commonwealth of Pennsylvania Council on the Arts.

This edition has been translated with the financial assistance of the Spanish Dirección General del Libro y Bibliotecas of the Ministerio de Cultura.

Contents

Sand

A Man Called Jeza

At the end of 1934, on a rainy calendar holiday, a man called Alejandro Zarco (friends, acquaintances, and even enemies called him Jeza) arrived at the island. His mission was to observe Party activities that weren't flourishing in that zone. Jeza was a tall, thin man, with prematurely white hair and blue eyes. Very few men happened to know him: Jose Taronji and the two brothers, Simeón and Zacarias. He hadn't come to the island to be an activist, his mission was simply to analyze and to report back to the Central Committee in Madrid and set up a plan to increase activities. When the war broke out a year or so later, José Taronji and the two brothers got involved in one of the first government dragnets. He later sent messages to the Party Central Headquarters via Herbert Franz, who was returning to his own country. He requested instructions and liaison procedures. Later, stokers, sailors, and stewards from Italy came to the island and made contact with Alejandro Zarco.

Perhaps one of these meetings had been broken up by the police. It seemed the police had set up a stakeout in the port, where the last meetings had been held. One afternoon, on February 5, 1937, the police surprised them and Alejandro Zarco was imprisoned. The sun was still shining, and a few fishing boats were leaving port. The women were spreading their nets on the sand, and the water seemed calm and gentle like a sleeping animal.

Everything that moved him was falling, like a rain of sand, leaving him dry, intact. He felt like he was made of granite, weighing in vain on the earth. On the other side of the window, autumn was lying in wait, and summer was there colorless and humid. Far from there an invisible fire was burning the walls of the houses. "My son, answer me," repeated the Father Superior. For the first time Manuel looked at him. "I have nothing to say."

His own voice surprised him. He understood that he was free, that in everything that surrounded him there was a remote beauty, something forgotten, rotten, like the fallen leaves of the trees. It was the same old monastery, the one of his childhood; the Father Superior was the same one as before; and there, outside, the same sky grew pale.

"Manuel," the father called him by his name again. "Manuel, my son."

The father put a hand on Manuel's shoulder. Turning his head lightly to one side he looked at the hand. And, in that moment, with that very light contact, a faint stirring of wrath was kindled in him, ferocious, like a blaze of fire lit up inside him. Even the Father Superior's words were floating in front of his eyes like a will-o'-the-wisp, fugitive, zigzagging.

(Jorge de Son Major has died. Jorge de Son Major made a will. He recognizes you as the legitimate heir of his house and of all his belongings, and requires your presence at his funeral. At last Jorge de Son Major has made up for his mistake.)

"It's been a long time since they killed my father," said Manuel. "Right now, I don't understand anything else."

Two shrieking birds crossed each other outside the window. The father superior seemed startled.

"But my son, my son, my son...."

(I came across a man's broken and dismembered body, like a great and tragic puppet, on the sand, riddled with gunshot wounds.

The great doll, the tragic clown, so soon, obviously and clearly lying at my feet like this, in all its rawness. Poor José Taronji, who gave me my name, screaming into the sand, mute, sorrowful reproaches. His humiliated cadaver. Not even hatred could give him the strength to die when, at the last moment, he fled toward the railroad embankment below, trapped like a rabbit.) Now wrath seemed to become inflamed over the earth, out there in the sun that was soon to be nonexistent, it overcame him. Overcame him, Manuel (me, poor fellow that I always . was, poor devil, trapped, who was also me. Trapped, that's the word. The image haunts me, the memory of José Taronji, with his mouth open and his eyes staring glassily, dried blood on his shirt, face down in the sand, as though seeking shelter against the belly of the ship. I haven't forgotten it.)

"They killed him some time ago," he persisted. But this time his voice sounded bland, colorless. "I don't know who I have to honor at his funeral."

The Father's hand weighed more heavily on his shoulder. They were seated, as they had been so many times before, face to face, between the white-washed walls under the black cross made of cedar. (Manuel, Señor Son Major honors you with his esteem. Today he's sent you a new package of books. Give thanks to God that this noble señor gives you so much honor.) It was an ungoverned and immature joke, like a child's small ball that bounces from corner to corner.

"You were always good, Manuel. I never lost my confidence in you, you know that."

Manuel looked at his eyes with a cold curiosity. (I don't know that man.) His brown and hazel-colored eyes set in that small face, bundles of wrinkles, like nests of time, around his mouth. Two deep furrows went down from the point of his chin to where the low neck of his habit cut them off.

"Even when they carried me off to the reformatory?"

"We all redeem another's sins," the Father Superior replied. "All the elect. Don't you remember, Manuel? Wasn't it nice, Manuel? Maybe? Remember how you were, your own self, in this place, my son. When I used to say to you, 'Perhaps the Lord chose you to cleanse the sins of the earth.' Yes, Manuel, you were always good."

(An unknown man. The white cell, the crucifix, the empty nests hanging from the eaves above the open window, are more familiar then he is.) A long-lasting lethargy rose up, invaded by the cry of the birds, by voices of boys and the smell of burning leaves. (But my father has died. I picked him up from the ground. Poor José Taronji, death gave you your true measure.)

September's invisible fire took hold of the cloister, the velvety leaves that don't die, like a silent song of the earth.

"I'm speaking to you of your true father, Manuel. Thanks be to God, my son, justice was done. I've brought you out of there and I assure you won't go back there. Get ready to be worthy of your name..."

Manuel's smile stopped his flow of words.

"My father was murdered by the Taronji brothers, his relatives," he repeated with malign stubbornness." They gave me that for a father. I picked him up in *Doña's* Praxede's boat and carried him home. My mother washed off the body and the blood.... And she also combed his hair. I remember all that very well. She went to the closet and got out a clean shirt and took off his shoes. On the following day we buried him ourselves. Far away where nobody could be offended."

The Father Superior closed his eyes and crossed his two hands over his stomach. Something had appeared on the sides of his nose.

"Go, Manuel," he said. "Someone is waiting for you, outside these walls where no woman can enter. Go and be kind to her."

(She.) For a long time, he didn't know since when, whether from the time of the womb where he had begun to move, or from this very moment when the Father Superior had just spoken, saying, "Be kind to her," a dark rancor had been invading him, old and secret (such a rancor as the earth is supposed to feel against the thousand shapes that wound and bruise it, and those which, for a time, comfort it). A rancor, passive and without rage, not exempt from love, transformed him. He saw the trees shed their leaves, lose their bark. He, too, stripped himself slowly and inexorably of his credulous infancy, of the last heaviness of sleep. (The rancor, passive and without consequence, that precedes, perhaps, human love; a rancor that grows from the stars of the grass with magic regularity.) She, whom he could not blame for anything as a human being, but who was his flesh, his bones, his conscience, a living and breathing reproach. (I am not a good boy. I am a misguided and undisciplined child who doesn't follow the laws nor observe the marks of respect, or mourning, or joy, to the logical and decent mask of those irreproachable people who live here. I'm not a good boy, I'm an expert in truth. I'm an immoral nonconformist.) It has been a long time since I cried. Although he almost never cried (once, yes. I remember very well, when the swifts arrived unexpectedly at the door and cried out that life was waking up, and I didn't know it. I was only ten and was reading stories that claimed to define real life outside the walls of the monastery. I was wearing a brown serge outfit and the other boys were making fun of my red, Jewish hair. The Father Superior said "Jesus Christ also had red hair" and the children became silent. I felt infatuously exalted like a balloon on the verge of bursting through the clouds. I swallowed the bait of kindness like a stupid, fat fish swallowing the worm of his own death.) He looked at the Father Superior, the man who, perhaps up to this moment, he had most respected in his life. The Father was now talking about the death of his father. About death. (But no man is respectable, not even the saints, not even the madmen, not even the children who play with stones next to the wells, shouting out to one another, with innocent cruelty, thirsty for a heroism they don't know. No one is respectable up to this point, even though peace, love, and real life are announced.) (Love? What love?) Everything was torn up, dry, a crackling rain of sand above and around oneself, neither trampling down nor burning, not wetting or leaving any trace. Sand that returned to sand and remained thus, stretched out and terrifying, allowing itself to be devoured and returned to the beach with exasperating regularity. (The Father Superior used to say "death is resurrection." And I didn't know anything about life, or about death. I only knew about an obscure and timid respect for the people in my household, for José Taronji, who didn't love me; my mother; and the children, Tomeu and Maria. Death and resurrection, what could they be? Warm and golden ghosts above the brown bark of the earth, sown with roots and fireflies. In the center of the cloister there was a fountain with wide damp leaves and the Father Superior used to say, "Manuel, death is resurrection." And the day of the Resurrection of the Lord will arrive and the bells will ring out. The wind will press forward the friars' long habits and in his right hand the Father Superior will carry his dark laurel leaves that still hold their trembling drops. He kissed me and all the boys on the forehead and said, "Christ is risen." And nearby the smell of spring saturated with decay emerged. And Brother Gardener swept the leaves that an unexpected violent sea wind had torn from the branches. Everything was still soaked from the last storm. Even the bolts of lightning seemed hidden beneath the ground (the enormous and white crackling of the sky that our children's ears could foretell); and the thunder that rolled and rushed headlong even into the depths of the sea and the mountains that breathed in the orchard under our bare feet. Spring resounded, beautiful and excessive like the lime on the walls of the cloister in the sun. The earth resounded too, and it could be dug up to reveal putrid and gelatinous materials, germs of a life still frightening. The cloister, on the contrary, smelled like cinnamon, like the cake served on Holy Saturday. The children would hold out their hands and pottery bowls to get a piece of cake. The children were the sons and daughters of fishermen and peasants who sought instruction at the cost of shaved heads and lowered eyes. Something old and mystical emerged from the fountain in the center of the cloister; a little bit more, and everything, sweetish and cloudy like incense, also smelling of decay, like the heart of the earth. It was spring, and you could read at determined hours. He had sent me his travel books, always his travel books, his marine maps, his obsessive dreams about islands—a special treatise that gives great pleasure. Ah yes, those disturbing books that spoke of the spice-route and nocturnal caravans of boats at full sail in cavalcades above a sea of thirsty and phosphorescent sand. And beyond the cloister and poor children who wanted to be good, life groaned like an old cow. And I, wrapped in my brown serge habit with the olive branch between my fingers, used to say, "to be born again is glory, death is life.")

Manuel stood up. (Why does the evocation of childhood still move me, childhood which, in some way, is always happy? A dry desert in front of your eyes. Footprints in the sand, ghosts of steps that were easy to flee from, with the first wind.)

"When they took you off to the reformatory," the Father Superior said, "I said to myself, 'something horrible is happening, something which even I cannot overcome.' But Manuel, my son, the paths of God advance and cross each other back and forth; paths of shadows and of light that we, poor mortals, will never understand."

Once again it was the same voice, the same ideas, the same gestures. (Everything old, lost, the strength gone.)

Sand. Nothing.

"Go away," said the Father Superior. "Go through the door; leave. Your mother is waiting for you in the esplanade. Be kind to a poor woman, Manuel."

2

A poor woman advanced in years (her faded beauty bitterly paid for) has her head wrapped up in a black scarf. Perhaps two years are not sufficient for a woman's hair to return to its primitive beauty after having been shaved. A poor woman.

(The village women dragged her to the public square. Because you have become too insolent. Now I can't imagine her insolence, only the shining light of her eyes, of a burning blue-green in her frightened, white face, inexpressive from fear in the profane sun of the square. The sun that devastated the grass and men; that dried up insects and turned to ash the leaves that had fallen from the trees.)

She was outside on the esplanade, seated on one of the wooden benches the peasants had set up when they came on their carts from a pilgrimage. They had filled the grass with green bits of broken bottles, church tapers and ribbons, colored roses and greasy papers, all of which had to be walked on. She was sitting down looking at the ground with her hands crossed on her knees.

When I'd go home for Christmas, she'd be waiting for me at the gate of our family orchard on the slope covered with almonds and olives above the sea. She had the strange vocabulary of a village woman, "my lost lamb, my treasure," she'd say while scarcely smiling, yet with a vague smile that shone in her eyes, then on her lips. She was there, with all the light of winter around her, among the black trees, without birds, even without rain. She spread her arms, pressing me against her; and I experienced the smell of the wool of her dress, its rough contact on my skin, and the vague uneasiness that invaded me. I remember my shyness when faced with expressions of affection and irrational display of any kind of emotions; and my rough stupor for all human things. Because here, in the monastery, I lived away from it, in a great serenity. And, at that time, she kept fruit for me, which was also very unusual. She'd cut the fruit and peel the skin. "For my little friar," she used to say in her strange language, which disconcerted me, "he will wash away the sins of the world with his kindness." But I couldn't understand her. I used to just look at her and be astonished by her, her voice, the irritating beauty of her red hair around her white and arched forehead and her long eyelashes fluttering like golden butterflies. How strange she appeared to me, so

different from the other women I used to see. Blond eyelashes, bright
eyes, strange creature with clever hands and iridescent nails, such
unusual nails for a woman of the village. And the women of the village
dragged her to the center of the square. She has become insolent and
perhaps her strange language was for the women of insolence. And
they dragged her, like a rebellious goat being sent to the slaughter-
house. She had lost a shoe in the struggle and a white toe showed from
the torn stocking. It was almost obscene and ridiculous in the harsh
light of the afternoon falling on the dust of the square. A thread of
blood fell from the corner of her mouth because the blacksmith's wife
had slapped her. The blacksmith's wife used to say, "A warning, that's
what had to be done. A warning to people of that sort, people like her."
And she defended herself without hope or courage, but with a passive
tenacity like that of a quietly stubborn animal, undaunted, unaware of
its own solemnity. And the children came to my house and yelled,
"They're going to beat Sa Malené, the women want to give Sa Malené
a beating." And I ran out of the house toward the square and the
confusion of the violent group of women dressed in black. The
blacksmith headed me off, the smell of his apron against my face and
the hardness of his arm crossed against my stomach and pressed me
against the wall to keep me from running past. "Be quiet, boy, these
are women's affairs. Stay there," he said. "Look at me, I'm a man,
aren't I? Don't you think I'm a man? Then don't get me involved in
women's affairs. Quiet, quiet." And he pushed me against the way
even more as he looked at me with his little squinty eyes. In them I
suddenly discovered a savage sadness, a desperate sadness that came
from far away, that resembled hatred; something passive and so deep
that a man's body can bear it without an infinite fatigue. And the
woman took off her head-scarf and undid her braid which she had
wrapped around in a bun. I had seen her braid and unbraid her hair so
many times when I was a boy, when I still looked at her sitting on the
bed and she used to comb her hair in a leisurely and childish ritual,
something so beautiful and new every day, similar to the business of
birds on the eaves of the roof. "Be kind to this poor woman," the Father
Superior had just said. But it is possible that kindness might surprise
her because, as I understand it, no one had ever been kind to her. And
with a brutal shove they pushed her to the ground on her knees. Laughs
and cries and an acid happiness, implacably feminine; they brought

some big shears used for shearing sheep. And there were a couple of girls, too. One of them was called Margelida, with a black, thick, shiny braid hanging down her back, her eyes round and searching, filled with a thirsty curiosity. She must have been twelve or fourteen years old, with aggressive breasts pressing her much-too-tight blue blouse; her legs were solid and impatient. And the other one behind her was smaller, like a skinny, little dog. And the two shrieked with the irritating sound of a file against a grindstone. And in their fists they grasped, like golden snake, the braid of the poor woman for whom I must now feel kindness. Like shiny ribbons in the sun those two girls held the loving braiding and unbraiding that I had contemplated in the past—perhaps I was three or four at the most—sitting on the bed as her reflection shown in the black mirror of the dresser. And as the girls carried off the burning locks in their fists, I saw her arms, in the past, high above the back of her neck; I saw them in the sun like golden dust. Her mouth, bristling with black hairpins used to strike me with terror when she'd laugh with them between her teeth and I wouldn't understand what she was saying. The black teeth of the comb were the foreshadowing of something ferocious and gratuitous, under that same sun which, suddenly, had become female, voracious as an idol, blood-thirsty and abusive like the women in the square. "No one is good," the Father Superior used to say. The most saintly saint sins seven times a day; while I, a child in the serge outfit, would go about gathering fruit from the orchard with the brother in charge of it. And I used to say to myself, "No one is evil. A dull boy, red-haired like the devil, like Jesus Christ, depending on how they wanted to look at me, under what sun and what light, a poor boy who gathered vegetables and spied on, as if seeing an illusion, the flowering of the very white gardenias in the Father Superior's little garden. A boy who would run like a puppy chasing bees or butterflies or a piece of silver-foil—the kind that remains forgotten like foolish stars in the grass after pilgrimages— toward the father and cry out, 'Father, they have already appeared, the gardenias have already sprouted!'" And meanwhile, my hands would grab the grating of the green iron fence; and I felt my heart there, on the iron railings, like a mute bell. "No one is evil," he used to say to me as I held my raffia basket filled with green heads of lettuce, red tomatoes and orange-colored carrots while following behind the bare and callous feet of the Brother Gardener.

The color of the earth was mysterious and attractive like a story. The world, with all its pain, was beautiful because the pain was like an incense that could upset me. And I thought that the brothers would keep me in some way. And the Father Superior used to say, "You should understand that pain is good, that the bark of the world is made only of selfishness." And there, in the square, the woman remained alone, on her knees, beaten, with her half-bare skull. Locks of clumsily chopped hair, like ineptly mowed grass, sprang from it. There she was, splotched with red locks of hair and cries of laughter, which were also locks of some invisible fire, unintelligible even for me. The blacksmith removed his arm from around my stomach and said, "Go, go home. Believe me it's for your own good, go home, my son." That day, he called me "my son," like José Taronji, dead of gunshot wounds, used to call me; like the abbot called me, like that poor woman who slowly got up from the ground, first onto one knee, then the other, and who raised one trembling hand up to her ravaged neck, called me; and that hand had remained for a while, perplexed, in the lukewarm emptiness of her head, like a bird whose nest has been destroyed by a storm. But Jorge de Son Major never called me "my son." So why now? What could bring us together? What invisible bond reaches up to me, across death, drowning me?

Sa Malené, lit up by the last splendor of the evening, sat motionless on the bench under a fig tree.

"Mother," I said.

She turned around to look at me, shyly, and stood up. She had a handkerchief clutched in the fist of her right hand. It was something so typical of her, that long, white point, hanging like a damp wing, that all at once my childhood spent in the house on the slope came back to me. I embraced her in silence and she raised her hand, touched her head, and then let it fall behind her hair.

"Are you all right?"

"Yes, I'm very well."

"I've never written you because, what was I going to say to you? I didn't know whether my letters would reach you here, or that they'd even be given to you. You already know—I'm an ignorant woman. I have never been able to keep some things quiet. You already know me, I'm not able to keep silent at times. For that reason...."

He saw that her eyes were shining, almost like those of a girl, in that withered face. Those eyes, that innocence that was in spite of itself, almost pathological and it irritated him.

It was like a disease, her purity in evil, her passivity in affliction.

"Let it be, mother," he said. "It's better this way. I didn't want to know anything about anybody."

She twisted the handkerchief as she nervously spoke. "Manuel, we have never spoken clearly, you and I, but you knew that, didn't you?"

She raised her head and looked over the trees and the green dome of the monastery at the reddish sky.

"What, Mother? That José Taronji was not my father? That my father was Jorge de Son Major?"

She appeared frightened. Perhaps because she had never heard him speak like that before.

"But now he admits it," she stammered.

"Mother, don't you remember any more? Have you already forgotten it? I brought you the corpse of José Taronji and together we went and buried it."

Sa Malené raised a hand as if to cover her mouth.

"Keep quiet, son.... Listen! Listen to this other thing. Forget your past."

Suddenly I felt I didn't love her. (Neither her nor my memories, nor the gardenias that flowered unexpectedly after I had already despaired that they wouldn't bud. I didn't love anything or anybody.) And I said, "I don't have a past."

I don't have a past. They say to a child, "this man is your father." And they kill him. And a different man has his servant call the child and say to him, "Come and be with an old man who really loves you, and forget the family, the parents, and the brothers I gave you." Leave everything and be with this poor old man. Forget your brothers for the sake of this poor old man." This is a past? I was a good boy. Everyone said so, "you're too good." And they blamed me for what I hadn't done, and they sent me to a reform school because I wasn't respected, I wasn't one of them. Nevertheless, they call me now, because my father was not the one who was tainted, because my brothers were not tainted, because my family is not the one which the kindly gentleman has assigned to me. My family, now, is only the cadaver of that man who sent me to his servant, like the devil among the olive trees, so he could tell me, "leave your family, come and keep company with my señor, who loves you well." Books, gifts, dreams of travel.. I want to become distinguished and make enemies. I don't have a past history. This is not a past history, it is something ugly, long and dark, with a hundred legs, like a caterpillar.

"Mother, I don't want anyone. I'm nothing."

"My son, my son," she replied, "I never understood you when you spoke, God knows that very well. At times it seemed to me that you used a strange language. At times you have too much education for a poor old woman like me. But now less than ever am I able to understand you, Manuel. Less than ever... We are poor, Manuel. Your brothers are hungry."

At that moment the flame went out and I felt alone again because of her indifference.

"It's all the same to me, mother," I said submissively. "I'll do what you want."

She wrapped her arm around his neck and drew him toward her. She was crying, with a cry of relief (she surprises me, in the same way the leaves of the fig tree or the color of the sky do).

"This is my son," she said to him. "This is my Manuel."

3

In the center of the church something black, long and sumptuously macabre arose, lifted high so that everyone could see it. Narrow and irreparable all around it, the gold on the black grew pale, and the artificial sun rays that splashed the darkness from one side to the other like reeling spiders were only ghosts of some other splendor. A large cushion of black velvet was waiting in vain for his head. Death was there as if it were being served at a banquet in which all must participate.

In the center facing the altar, was his prie-Dieu, tempting and voluptuous like a throne. Twelve enormous candelabras of carved wood held up large tapers which burned quietly and passionately like tongues that had been torn out. (The devil in person used to come to his banquet wrapped up in a cape of black velvet, his eyes behind dark glasses, Es Mariné used to say. Es Mariné, Sanamo, where are both of you now? Where were you relegated to in this celebration, you who had not given up loving him? But love, like the scattered ashes of the cemeteries, where does love go? Where is the smoke of love going to stop, the invisible and black particles of burned up love? Es Mariné, Sanamo, only you loved him and now no one has made a place for you in this last wedding banquet. These are your lord's wedding ceremonies, finally the old bachelor has celebrated espousals worthy of him. Stories, legends that the two of you used to tell me, malicious old men, in the refuge of a silence that was worse than iron collar of a pillory on a child's neck. Cursed be all of them, him and you for your tales and your ghostly boats, for your cursed islands.) And the wind came from up there, moaning, uttering something. (I've heard it said that the organ of Santa Maria is famous, a burning wind, something torrid that went from burning to freezing almost without transition. When will I be able to rid myself of the cloister, the monastery, the islands, love, when?) Something like the wind impelling an enormous, metallic sugar cane plantation, through which the storm of some dark and devastating world might have begun to blow impiously, making all the islands tremble and the earth and the water vibrate. Glass factories, too, with Saint George and the Martyrs, seemed to move back and forth in the inhuman sound, not born of men, but of some other place (to which we all sail, located here in the stone boat with yellow; in a ghostly ship, a sailboat that does not leave a trace nor any furrow in spite of sailing in the excessively dry sand; because that ship only navigates toward that something else, obscure and terrible, that we fend off like a black and incomprehensible sign. Because he's not here, the one who sent presents to the monastery. He's not there, the one who's evasive, proud, aloof, indifferent like the palm trees rocking next to the adobe wall of his house. His body isn't here, ardently sad, gratuitously sad, hatefully sad, he who sowed disorder in the children's consciences, children like me, like that poor and vile Borja, like that little girl called Matia, both of whom had disappeared the way I had disappeared and who wander about who knows where with what destination, toward what island of sand; and, like me, once grown up, are different, alienated. Jorge de Son Major has died, not now, but some time ago in the ashes of the Delfin. Only now has he returned to earth, as butterflies and dead otters, dead poppies and dead swallows return; like physical and beneficial death that feeds the earth and like life that treads upon our steps. The whole earth is wounded by footsteps that were footprints of feet already gone by, stones of a certain splendor that still remains. A splendor like this church—what hands, under what order of these walls were these walls raised, these windows—and those men and women there, now, behind me, pray-ing, with their brothers dead, humbled and despised, now here on their knees, thinking only of their business affairs, of their obligations, perhaps of their death; the death that was or the death that will be. The wind kept dashing at them, over their heads, moving them to and fro in their apathy or fear, their sadness, their gluttony.)

Manuel knelt (as poor José Taronji had done his whole life.) He felt the softness of the velvet on his knees. And then the three figures appeared, black and gold, shining, solid, three huge idols advancing softly, almost as though they weren't walking. A few children dressed in black velvet, like magnificent devils with long hoods over their backs from which hung tassels of gold, swayed their thuribles of death back and forth the way the wind shifts coming from above. An old and sweetly faded odor came up to him (the gardenias had bloomed; I contemplate myself drowning and floating like a shipwreck; and my skin, my eyes, my ears breathe their fragrance.) It's like a wine slightly mixed with my sense of smell, evaporating and disseminating like fog among the columns. The incense is red.) Then, in the choir, the voices arose above and behind their heads (it is the voice I had as a child, the voice of my childhood in the cloister, rebounding like luminous insects on the stones of the nave. The window pane fitted with lead, the wind in the immense and wild sugarcane plantation, the choir boys; and that death, there, long and black with its big cushion of black and gold velvet, moves forward between candelabras rising like golden trees. It moves forward, all of us move forward in the great wind of this boat, or of this monstrous mariner whose ribs I can count against me, like a cage, slowly and elusively, there where I don't want to go, where I have never wanted to go. Through this great dark sea, through this sea of dark mouths that open and close at my back, on my sides, through the sea of hypocritically veiled eyelids, among whistles coming from carnivorous teeth, begging for something destined for their very own gullets and fangs. Perhaps the incense is red, the sky, red; the night, too, when a storm threatens; like the moon on the night before a gale which lies on an indecipherable sea. A sea which encloses me and impels me toward that place where I have never wanted to be.... And I know so, for that boy still lives in me who ran down the orchard on the slope, where those whom everyone thought were my brothers awaited me; arms full of packages and Christmas presents; down the slope as I cried out the names of my brothers, "I want to be with you, this is my family!" And she used to say, "Son, you are too good." Why was I too good? If I didn't know, if it didn't seem to be so....I never thought so. "No one is good. No one is evil," my heart used to say when I was nine as I beat against the abbot's rail fence and peeked out at an astonished spring where the blossoming of the white flowers was a symptom of the indubitable goodness of nature. But, now, kneeling here I know, ("Son, you are too good." Not even that, "No one is good, no one is evil," words without meaning.) He looked around and suddenly heard the insolent call of Sa Malené. (What importance could good or evil have? The world was designed in another mold, built hammer blow by hammer blow, nail by nail, adjustment by adjustment, in accordance with another plan. Very soon they showed me that the world has other directions, it has a different framework.) Without fear and without goodness, he looked at those around him and saw them kneeling, as though lying in ambush waiting for something that was going to happen suddenly or within a great deal of time; or perhaps it was only a great desire or fear of what might happen. Beside him, empty, was the prie-Dieu of Jorge de Son Major's cousin, *Doña* Praxedes. (At least she, who hated him, was coherent and death has not tamed her manner of feeling and being.) She had begged off because of an illness that was perhaps real. On the adjacent prie-Dieu was Jorge's cousin, Emilia. One could scarcely see her profile, indistinct and rosy as it emerged from her black veil. She appeared as an inform mass, impersonal, absent, wherever she might be. He turned his head to the right and something jolted him. From that time on, from those days on, he had never seen them again. There they were, both of them next to the mayor. The falcon profile of the older brother superimposed on the softer and rounder profile of the younger, like two faces on the same side of a medal. The Taronjis, the sound of their steps on the stones, the blackness of the uniform coats in the sun. The Taronjis, with the smell of ancient burnt flesh which was glowing, burning on the stones of the little square and mounting to their eyes and teeth and their thirsty fangs in their pale faces. The rims of their eyes, dark like the smoke of the resplendent and diabolically luminous burning flesh, a greasy smoke that adhered to their clothes and their cold and fixed smiles. The Taronjis, the fear, like the terrible smell of extremely old burnt flesh, the smell of extremely old cadavers, disinterred and burnt and from whose bare skulls emerged locks of hair from an old, rotten head. The Taronjis, behind their steps a distant roll of the drums smelled of wax between hands bound with rope; and something which was their own roll of the drums, their own enormous revenge and the long, black chain of their servile smile toward *Señor* Son Major and *Señora Doña* Praxedes and the Princes of the Church. The Taronjis, as in that summer's evening, with little Tomeu, who came running up from below the embankment, his lips white, unable to utter words. He raised his hands to me and I looked at him. Poor Tomeu, he was scarcely eleven when he said to me, "Manuel, Manuel, they have taken him away.... they dragged him and the others from the Port." He wasn't able to speak. I had to shake him by the shoulders for him to say something. At that moment he wanted to be a man. He looked to me as the only man he knew who could protect him. Me, who had just reached sixteen and who stammered, "The Taronjis, who, Tomeu? The Taronjis?" A name that reaped heat and shade, sun and the soft flow of breathing. When I went to her and saw her stretched out on the bed with her arm across her eyes, I said to her, "Don't be afraid, nothing bad is going to happen to you, they only want to interrogate him." But she raised her head. And in her eyes was an old and fixed desperation that went through my chest and enraged me. Ah, the Taronjis, passing through the silent back alleys, at the dead hour of the sun, when the terror of their steps penetrated the windows. Then men and women interrupted their chores. They raised their hands on high and their smiles froze and their fear rose. Only the dogs dared bark at them from a distance, like José Taronji's little dog that went out into the road. His howl was long, wailing and challenging, like the omen of an inhuman vengeance that, someday, could break out.) The mayor, his wife, the councilman, to his left and his right; very soon, the brother, with all of them, would lower their heads in front of the incense of the world as though the crackling of the calcinated bones couldn't be heard anywhere nor the wailing cry of the dog that expressed his protest with his eyeballs in flames. As if nothing of all that were still burning some place, in some consciousness, he still remained kneeling in the prie-Dieu that waited in the church in vain, Sunday after Sunday, for the presence of its master, Jorge de Son Major. He was there on the gold prie-Dieu that still belonged to him, with all its past magnificence, and presided over this great farce. (What am I doing here, how is it possible for me to be here, in this way, kneeling, who am I honoring? I was already growing in Sa Malené's womb when he sent her from his house and married her off to José. I was growing in Sa Malené's womb when José carried her off to his house. And when I was born, he would bend over me to see how I was sleeping, just the way Malené would say to me, "so often, when he would work at night and stay for a while, he would look at you while you slept. Then he got all those ideas about Zacarias, Simeón, and all of them. Once you were sound asleep he would look at you and say, 'it would be something if this were the one who would one day avenge me"— and now, there he is, under the ground, mingling his ashes with those of so many who, like him, are calling from the ground. And I am kneeling here, in the presence of a death that doesn't bring anything to the great confusion, to the great thirst that consumes me. The whole town is here, that same town that they trod on, mixed with the one who trod on it. All are here, suddenly, like myself; behind me, a town lurking and looking on, a tame and indistinct dragon that was guarding something, partly satiated, partly hungering. Something perhaps that it does not yet know what it is, because the blood is still running from its fangs; but there is curiosity in its eyes, and simple emotion, the troubled stimulation of the organ and the children's angelic voices. They were all there, those who corrupted and the corrupted, those who destroyed and the destroyed, those who oppress and the oppressed, all together and kneeling the way I was, meditating about something, about someone. When will this finish? Who will rise up against this? Death, nothing more, here, in some and in others, suffocating stench of wax candles, incense and humanity crowded together under the violent wind of the organ, in the face of the death of the one who was indifferent. Meditating, seated at the door of his shops in order to trade in something, up to the point of trading in his own pain and his own humiliation. Where are the men? seated now, waiting for the hour of their spoils, easily and opportunely. Meditating about the voices of the children, about the music, about the forbidden gold of the church, about me.

Manuel got up, without haste, even though he felt all their eyes fixed on him, except for the distant ceremony of the three arrogant figures in gold and black velvet who moved smoothly at the altar, with courtly and delicate bows to one another. They raised their vestments gently to place them with great care on the backs of their benches. Undaunted, they carried on their rite of death. They kept on with their voices that translated the anguished cry of the dead, while he slowly turned toward the people and moved forward among them, dividing the tide. He went directly toward the closed door covered with gold and black velvet, between the flames of all twelve candelabras. Only the flames seemed cut off, tongues that wanted to cry out something, as though impelled by the great sugar cane field. He moved forward without saying anything, not turning his head even once toward the terrible banquet, toward the black, closed, inhuman thing that rose in the center of the nave. (Outside there was the sun. Through the curtain and the iron roses on the door, there was the dust where I had to suffer so much. Even now there is no remedy for a child's suffering, the suffering of a poor oppressed boy; nor for the wanderings of a boy who asked for work from door to door; nor for the doors that closed when I went by; nor for the arms that refused to give me help. Nothing of all that has any meaning, or any feeling whatsoever for anybody.) He stopped for a moment in front of the curtain. At that moment the music ceased. A solemn voice rose up over the sea. Someone sat up on the benches and turned around to look at him. (It's like the sea itself, closing behind the boat.) Some hissing noise danced awkwardly in his ears. He pulled the curtain firmly and opened the door, heavy and creaking. And the sun, like an animal that had been waiting for too long, entered all at once. The gold seemed to go out and the sword of the voice, black and high, shattered. A grey cat, creeping along softly on its belly toward the baptismal fountain was blinded by the sunlight. The door closed once again behind his back.

Water kept springing from the fountain, the steep side-street, the stone steps. He went away from there and sought the path that led to the outskirts of the town beyond the mayor's house, toward the oak grove. And suddenly, as he left behind the walls of the houses, the windows and the gardens and remained alone with the sky and the distant trees, he broke into a run. He ran with savage terror, with red ants running through his arteries, and with a dehumanized fear that made him tremble and sweat. Something like a dark roar was following him. Until once again, after a great length of time, he found himself among the trees. The oak trees are there, as always, old friends, dauntless and coherent. José Taronji was there, dead and under the earth, between those two trunks, where the light entered without hurting the eyes (his ill-treated bones, sorry residue, enormous puppet forgotten on a dunghill.)

He didn't approach the tomb. From a distance he looked at the piece of ground where thorns, brambles and the lavender and white flowers of the woods were growing once more.

4

"I will take care of all your things, Manuel," Mossen Mayol said. "You don't have to worry. Come here, my son."

Once more, "my son." Suddenly everyone was addressing him that way. Mossen Mayol looked at him from the heights of his golden eyes. "I understand your feelings," he went on. "You have to make an effort to learn to carry this burden on your shoulders. Let's go, boy, don't be afraid, come with me."

On another occasion, in front of the closed fence of Son Major, the broad leaves of the palm trees moved in the wind. The sea could be heard on the cliff. (The wind always lashing like a persistent ghost.)

"Please," said Manuel, "I want to be alone."

He took the key from Mossen Mayol's hands and saw the offended amazement of his eyes. He pushed the door open and entered. The gravel crackled under his feet. The enclosed balcony was up there, its window panes shining, enclosing a disembodied shadow. Sanamo appeared in the corner of the house dressed in greenish-black. He shone like a blue stone in his indescribable sailor's cap. He came running up, as was his custom, with the footsteps of an old elf.

"Manuel, dear little dear, sweet little thing, finally you're coming home. Do you remember, dear? Do you still bear old Sanamo in mind, or are you going to cast reproaches at me?"

"Where were you going?" asked Manuel.

Mossen Mayol felt hoarse.

"Well...."

He looked at him (it's an old and forgotten portrait.)

"Good-bye."

Mossen Mayol turned half-way around and left. His eyes had a shining brilliance, like burnished copper.

"Go there," Sanamo pointed away with his finger. He ran silently to the rail fence where he pressed his face so he could see him go down the road, leading to the bottom of the cliff. "Ah, understand. The *Señor* didn't want to see you around here, Manuel, my little bird, you have become a little unfriendly."

They climbed the staircase, one against the other (like two pals returning from school.)

"Before this you were sweet as a honeycomb."

"Sanamo," he said. "Please stop talking this way."

"Ah! Ah! you are no longer a child."

"Well, then don't forget it."

Sanamo began to laugh.

The house smelled like waxed wood. With its white slipcovers, the old furniture looked like heavy, concrete ghosts, weighing without mystery on the carpet. Family portraits, blue uniforms and dark frock-coats, red medals, statuettes of jade and ivory; Manuel raised his hand to his eyes.

"Don't cry," said Sanamo, "Life is like this."

"Do you want to shut up once and for all? I'm not crying."

"Not crying?"

"I'm horrified. Nothing more."

"What a way to talk!"

(How can you understand me, Sanamo? I am afraid because of what I was about to become.)

Sanamo shrugged his shoulders and opened his arms. Then he ran to open the curtains. (The muffled sound of the velvet, the pink light on the gilt of the frames; the grand piano, old, astute and dull lurking in the shadows; the lamp of a thousand tapers, the cobwebs that shine, almost of gold, once again in front of me.) Sanamo's rapid steps made the Venetian glass tinkle. Sanamo began to slap the big cushions the way a woman does when punishing her child.

"I have come here every day to pray," he said. "In my own way, you know. And I have my prayers."

"You didn't go to the funeral?"

"No. What's the point? I was here, with the guitar."

The cushions emitted a pungent dust that evoked the past. (I used to come here for Christmas. I used to put on the navy blue suit with silver buttons that he sent me. I took off the serge outfit and the sandals I wore in the monastery. He used to invite me to dinner. The sun shined here, in this room, and I wanted to know so many things about him, about his statuettes and pagan gods, about his bell-glasses with their asphyxiated sailing ships, and captured ships, in a cankered crystal bottle. Father, why hast thou forsaken me?

"And I have a lot of things to show you, son of the falcon." Sanamo was speaking. "Prince of my house, my heart."

"Sanamo, enough, don't speak to me like that." He might have had a lot of fun with it, but I didn't.

Sanamo creaked about in the corners, opening shutters, standing on tiptoe like a gnome. His laughter meshed with the squeaking of the hinges. (Old malignant man, how I once feared you and loved you, you too, obscurely, when you made up songs. Where did you go to get your embroidered cap from Corfu with its long tassel? You poisoned me with your stories as he did with his silence. Everything here trapped, clouded bell-glasses, green empty bottles. Poor asphyxiated sailboats, all of it has become a thousand bits and pieces of crystal, the sails have already straggled off. How can one do all that to a child? The poison of lies is sweeter than the poison of truth. I am being reborn from the malefic exorcism. Old perverter of innocent hearts, you must change your way of speaking.) Manuel sat down on the divan with white and yellow flowers from India (it smelled of musk and myrrh) and began to break into laughter. Sanamo ran up to him, his arm outstretched.

"Do you remember the buried prince, the one with the silver turban destined to die? He cut the melon with his golden dagger, and the very same dagger fell upon his chest and split his heart. How he made you weep as a child!"

Manuel kept laughing, his hands on his knees, his head down. It was a noiseless laughter that shook his shoulders with an invisible clap of thunder.

"Do you remember our stories? Look, you would come from outside there, you'd sit down with your legs crossed and you'd say, "Tell me Sanamo, what happened to the Prince afterward?" Ah, how I wanted to say to you, "You are the prince." But I was afraid the falcon would hear me. I didn't have permission to reveal secrets. Manuelito, I'm also afraid. I remember that golden dagger, the one that split the heart of the poor boy."

Manuel kept on laughing. He raised his hands to his eyes. It was a dark hand, heavy and powerful.

Manuel took his hand away from his eyes and looked at him. Sanamo pulled back a step.

"Your eyes are two wild beasts... what have they done to you, Manuel? Where did they take you that they have changed you this way?"

"Get me some wine."

Sanamo disappeared and returned with the bottle and two glasses.

"Are you going to let me drink, too?"

"Do whatever you feel like doing, Sanamo. You always did that before, didn't you?"

The pink wine filled the glasses.

Sanamo clacked his tongue and began to hum a little tune. Manuel, in his memory, followed the tune, like the wake of a ship. He drank.

"Did they make you work a lot?"

"I'm used to it."

"Were they tough?"

"Like everybody."

"What was worse? To be shut up?"

(The worst, to be paying for a mistake.) He shrugged his shoulders and Sanamo filled up his glass again.

"Your mother," he said hesitating, "is she going to come live here too?"

A controlled hatred trembled in the old man's voice. (He always detested my mother. And my brothers. What an unusual and corrupt faithfulness this one has. Everything hangs together here. Except for me. I'm like an arrow that has disappeared outside the bull's eye, an arrow shot with force, deflected. Except for me. I've been flung far away, now, finally.)

"No, nobody is going to live here except you. Be assured none of us will bother you."

Sanamo fell on his knees. (It's still extraordinary, his nimbleness, even now.) He wrapped his arms around the other one's knees.

"Not you, not you," he shrieked. He saw his eyes, desperate, flooded with a mixture of panic and wild joy. "How are you going to live far from here? Where will you live?"

"Not here."

Sanamo unfolded his arms from around Manuel's knees, looking up at him from the floor.

"Where are you going to live?"

"Where I always have, on the slope, with my mother and my brothers. Now they will not be hungry."

Sanamo shrugged his shoulders.

"What do you want? Most of the people in the world experience hunger. It's always been that way. Me too, I experienced a lot of hunger as a child. Look at my body, do you think I grew up normally, do you think that I developed and grew up the way one is supposed to? I was a wreck when he put me on another track," he kept saying to him with irrefutable meaning, almost eternal.

"Good bye, Sanamo."

"Where are you going?"

He followed him with a strange haste; he could not state precisely whether impatiently because he was leaving, or painfully because he was leaving him.

"You'll come back? I have to show you something, something that belonged to the *Señor* and which you'll like. You know? Finally he had bought a boat again. What a beauty!"

"Where is it?"

"In the Port. Es Mariné keeps it hidden in the landing. You remember, under the terrace…. that is very much controlled now. But he had permission to do anything. And I wonder, what are we going to do with the boat now? Really, it's a pretty Mallorcan boat with a motor, very spacious. Let's go for a sail together. On occasions he would go with me, on other occasions with Es Mariné or alone. But now, what am I supposed to say to you? The war is coming to an end, you can almost say that it is over with, it's won. And these things are no longer of serious concern. I believe that they will let you go out with her because now you are his only son, really and truly."

Manuel had remained immobile and Sanamo became alarmed.

"What's going on with you? Why are you looking at me this way? Have I said something that might offend you?"

At three-thirty in the afternoon he went out in Sanamo's boat, and around four he arrived at the Port. To the right was the little beach of Santa Catalina, with its abandoned boats. He contemplated the brilliance of the sun on the golden shells, the agave plants and the green reeds. The beach was not only a cemetery for the boats but also for something, something that he had kept in his mind for a long time and that now lay mute, dead, imprisoned in the dryness of the sand.

There it was, the rocky coast, dotted by grottoes and the houses almost superimposed above the landing. Its long narrow ladders of wood were black from so much humidity. (The Port, so many memories, José Taronji, Jeza, and the brothers Simeón and Zacarias.)

More to one side, more out into the sea, above a projecting shelf over the cliff appeared Es Mariné's "El Café," which was at one time a beautiful house. There only remained the extravagance of the balustrade, pink, long, on the broad terrace of the destroyed beauty. The stained walls, with names carved into it by the point of a knife. Boys' names, names of men, who gathered together there to drink, play or eat before going to work or to plan adventures on a slow Sunday afternoon as the dust rose on the distant land used by carts. Es Mariné's café, where men used to get together to chat, drink wine and play cards on Sunday mornings, on Saturday nights. Nests of smugglers, fishermen, dreamy young men who carved their names on the wall, with a vague desire for immortality. In Es Mariné's little landing, under the great vaulted terrace is where Sanamo said they kept the "Antinea".

He tied up the boat and jumped. Two women sitting on the ground, reddened under the sun, were working on their nets. A puppy was sniffing in the trash somewhere under the rocks. It smelled like rotten fish, like dung. Someone had placed a row of flower pots in which scarlet geraniums were growing. The women were barefoot. He contemplated the stretched out feet of the youngest woman, the soles of her feet crisscrossed with furrows. They were dark feet, almost black against the sand. He walked over the rocks toward Es Mariné's café. Suddenly it seemed to him that he had gone back in time (an enormous leap backward and he caught in mid air the uncertain and shaky loose end of a moment in time, and it came back to me.) But, in all of that, there was present a harsh, rough reality that made things stand out, made the countryside stand out in almost sad contours. He pushed open the French door and the odor of mold and sausages and olives overcame him. Es Mariné's shop-café-refuge-lair was there, his dwelling, his past, his present. To the right the long wooden counter, the rolls of fishing lines, the iron cages with their parrots and, straight ahead, the other door, arched, which surprisingly, was open to the green light of the sea like an imprisoned firmament. A restless, sad calm lay on everything. Only the parrot Mambrú got upset and rolled his cruel, almost human eyes.

A body, the high shoulders, the heavy head of Es Mariné emerged from the shadow. He remained standing firmly in front of

Manuel. Es Mariné stood with his back to the light; Manuel couldn't see his face, only the burning red of the end of his cigarette.

"Manuel," he said, "I knew that you were going to come, boy."

He held his hand out to him after having rubbed it against his leg. Mambrú began to scream something and Es Mariné moved toward the counter.

"What do you want to drink?"

"Whatever there is."

He noticed that his palate was dry, a mixed emotion, not concerned with Son Major, and which had nothing to do with either his childhood or with his former pain, overcame him.

"Marine, I want to talk to you."

Es Mariné's hand remained suspended in the air. (He was afraid to remember or feel something that he didn't want to.)

"Nothing in particular," he explained. "Just chat, nothing else."

"I understand."

Es Mariné took out a big-bellied black bottle.

He took out two small glasses and filled them with a thick yellow liqueur. Then he threaded the glasses between his fingers and with a notion of his head indicated that he should follow him.

The terrace was the same as always, chipped, and the wooden tables, on trestles, were covered with grease spots....the rolls of fishing lines, the pots of tar, the piles of cans and boxes.... the spread out calm and hard like zinc surface under the green paleness of a sky that seemed to recede, to become convex in an infinite vertigo. There were no clouds. There, to the right, floated a very transparent cloud. They sat down, one in front of the other and drank.

Everything was the way it was before, just like three, five, or ten years earlier. Nothing had happened. (Nobody has died. Nobody is living. Only the sea breathes and laps inexorably at the edges of the earth, at the pillars under the terrace, and, if Sanamo hadn't lied, at the sides of the "Antinea".

"Marine," he said finally. "What became of all of them?"

Marine remained very quiet, with his enormous tilted head.

"Who?"

"Jeza, and the two brothers, Simeón and Zacarias."

"You still remember them, Manuel? Drop it, believe me. All of that is over with, in the past. Look, I've heard that you're coming along with a different kind of life now. That's the way he was. Perhaps he didn't behave himself well with you ... with Sa Malené, I mean. But Manuel, in the end he was good. Respect his memory, I tell you he was a great gentleman. Keep all the respect and affection you can for him. Believe me, believe this old man who knows something about life."

"I have not come to talk about Jorge de Son Major, Marine. I want to talk about José Taronji, Jeza and the two brothers."

"Forget all that, Manuel," Es Mariné cried out, pounding on the table. "Forget them once and for all or get out of here!"

Suddenly it seemed to him that Es Mariné had changed, that he was not the same old sailor, irritable and steady, faithful and coherent in his memories. He was a scared man. But there was an enormous sadness in his eyes, in his glance, like a thief. His voice trembled when he said, "Manuel, you already know that I was their friend. You know it very well, better than anyone. This house was their house. I was very fond of Jeza. But I was more fond of Jorge than anyone else. Yes, I know what you're thinking. Secrets on both sides fool everybody. It's not like that, my son. Some I understood well, but I couldn't help liking the other. He was my life, years and years of my life with him, in the Delfin. And I wasn't going to stop liking him because he didn't understand his faults. But I did what I could for Jeza, for José Taronji." He suddenly had a seizure of fear, but he swallowed his saliva and added: "Although you might not believe it, although everyone blames me, I did it for you, Manuel."

"Show me where they used to get together. I want to see it again."

"Up there, on the hill." Es Mariné's voice changed into a hiss. "At times they got together here. But it wasn't here, thank God, that the butcher discovered them. It was there, in the empty house."

"I was there. I had gone to bring them dinner. They left me alone because I was only a boy then and because...."

"And because they knew that you were Jorge de Son Major's son." In spite of everything Manuel was still surprised at the pride that lay in those words.

(The butcher. The right arm of the Taronji. On Sundays he put on his new military tunic; his massive belly pushed out the buttons. He always had a cigar stub sticking out from his mouth. His wide belt climbed under his arms. For a long time he had been lying in wait for José Taronji, poor José, slow, devoted and doleful, with a gentle and imprudent tongue. Jeza didn't trust him. "José, you worry me," He used to say. I went to the abandoned house to take them their dinner. In those days the brothers and José Taronji were in hiding. They were afraid to be seen in the city. The butcher asked me maliciously, "And how about your father?" And I answered: "He's out of town, I think he went to Palma for some reason." On the following Monday he discovered the abandoned house. On that day he entered, followed by his older son...the black shine of his pistols, the heavy legs planted firmly on the ground, choleric, convinced, scandalized and no matter what is useless in this situation, useless in the anguished everyday struggle, the struggle of words that left a coat of sand on the palate, a dry wind that scratched, that laid waste. It made no difference. There he was, the little self-conscious man, sure of his immovable reason, hanging on the telephone, clamoring for the sword of justice against depraved hearts, hearts that were useless and unmoved by their fellow men—not his fellow men, needless to say. The wind continued outside, carrying off the murmur of the voices. Two or three times the wind beat against the window pane. Then I heard the metallic and vibrating sound of the electric wire, shaking. I remember the rows of dark birds with their little dead claws; they were in the habit of perching on the cables. "What has possibly become of them now?" They had fled, just like the days, the minutes. All that was necessary to carry them off was a gust of wind, a black, sudden wind that was enough to finish everything inside there. Everything fled, like spoken words, like birds. And that little man, the butcher, kept on, swollen with pride, with all the dignity of his being respectable, responsible, moral and to poor José Taronji, the two brothers Simeón and Zacarias he cried out "Don't move, you're caught!" There, on that beach, under that sun no longer shining, Jeza had spoken to me. The train would pass every morning on those same rails, and behind the train (I noticed only then how often the train passed, as if, until that moment, the horizon was only the black edge of the tracks), the wild stretch of sand with its thin, yellowing reeds lashed by the wind, and then the other sand, the bare, clean sand; the hard, compact sand of the beach. *All that has finished*; even though I might linger for days or months, I knew that everything was over with. A sharp whistle cut through the wind. I heard the jolting on the track, the broken panes vibrated and the train, once again, with all its windows burning, like a luminous worm, swift and yellow like phosphorescent and swift harmonicas, crossing the sand of the beach. I remember that the edges of the sea were shining. I looked through the pieces of broken glass, thinking, with all the strength that my heart was capable of holding, "Don't let Jeza come, don't let him get here, let something detain him. Let no one discover Jeza because, then, everything is lost."

A cold moon came from somewhere and drew near the edges of the sea, to the waves that never finished overtaking you; threatened, and only remained in sand, in foam. Only the sand and the wind were there, allied, moistening one another, at intervals. Behind the last railway car fled red flashes of light, like an advertisement or an appeal. "Let's go, on foot," said the little man. He wrapped himself up well in his black jacket and crossed it over his round belly, almost indecently, and slowly drew away from the door, all the while aiming his gun at them.

"You are the little friar, aren't you? Give thanks that you are a child, only a child who has come to bring food." At that moment, stridently, the shrill noise of the small door of the enclosure was heard. With a mechanical gesture he extended his hand toward the closed door of the house and left it suspended in the air before the anxious eyes of José Taronji and the two brothers. The chubby, pale hand carefully grasped the door knob. My heart turned over and I understood all the reality of what was going on. For that gesture had brought the whole catastrophe to me all at once. "It's Jeza. Now there's nothing to do about it. Jeza's in the trap, too." But it wasn't him, only José Taronji's faithful and howling puppy.)

"They took them away. On the following day the Taronji killed José, who tried to escape. But what about Jeza? Where is he?"

"They put him in jail this last February. He must still be there. They weren't interested in poor Taronji. Jeza was more important. I suppose they want to question him. I haven't heard anything about him again."

"And what about her, the wife?"

"I don't know," said Es Mariné. "Go on, Manuel, forget all about it. The war is ending any day now. Forget all those things."

Rain

Alejandro Zarco told his wife, "If something should happen to me someday, by all means try to deliver these documents to a man named Esteban Martin." A short time later he was imprisoned and his wife took refuge in the interior of the island. The wife was carrying the documents with her and hid them.

Alejandro Zarco lived as long as an exchange of prisoners was still a possiblity. In mid-October 1938 he was executed.

1

The bus had been parked for a while and was still rattling. From the window he saw the driver, in his dark green sweater, speaking agitatedly with the owner of the cafe. The little square shone in the absolutely savage sun in contrast with the restaurant signs, the small tables of round and cold marble, and the dust that the wind was raising somewhere over the bridge. That sun, an arid, dense ball, seemed to hold onto the sky like a mollusk. They had been there for more than ten minutes, for at least a quarter of an hour, detained in the square while the driver was speaking with the man from the cafe as the sun struggled with the end of the afternoon. Inside the bus the people were getting impatient. All of them, or almost all, were peasants, in black suits with their shirt-collars unbuttoned and not wearing ties. Women, men, impenetrable countenances and quiet eyes had a lustrous and hard brilliancy like the shell of certain insects. People who had come down to run errands for themselves or others, to have a tooth out, to sell, to buy. There was somewhat of an animal smell inside the bus, blurring the window panes.

The motor, in its wide chassis, complained obscurely until a doll that was hanging from the windshield trembled. The trees, dark brown and silver, faded against the sky. The cold season had arrived.

He turned his eyes away from the driver, away from the man in the cafe. On the red wall of the church a shining arrow, painted in white, pointed the way.

He half-closed his eyes. A slow heaviness slipped through his eyelids. And suddenly he saw them. Two women, right there in front of him, as though growing stiffly out of the ground. One stood in front of the other, both in black. There they were, looking at each other. Perhaps one of them was slightly moving her lips. One of them had her arm stretched out, her hand resting on the other woman's shoulder. They were two placid women, speaking and looking at each other. He had seen them days before, waiting in the prison courtyard. The hand, which lay on the other woman's shoulder, had something heavy about it, something confused and foundering... a quiet and dark hand, with thick fingers, heavy as a shovel, on the other woman's shoulder.

(I remember Jeza's arms. They were long, with somewhat prominent knuckles, golden brown in color, like the crust of bread.

Hard, useful hands. I almost always looked at his hands when I spoke to him. His hands revealed much more than did his face. And Jeza's hands had risen up now, the way these two women rose up from out of the heavy and compact earth, the dreadful earth, where his dead ones lay, to cry out to me. Jeza's hands were raised up from amid a feeling of heaviness between the two women in mourning. They were there, spread open, like a monstrous fan.)

He jumped from his seat, stumbled, and went toward the door of the bus. He was trembling like a coward.

A woman said, "Hey, look. All this time parked, and when the driver returns he decides to get off."

The driver suddenly threw his cigarette butt on the ground. He squashed it under his heel and returned to the bus. He rubbed his hands. They jostled against one another at the door.

"Let's go…"

He didn't pay attention. He got off the bus, like a dog that has been closed up and suddenly sees freedom.

The driver stuck his head out the window, shouting at him. The wind blew through his black and greasy hair. The women inside the bus made mute and stupid gestures, raising their hands on the other side of the blurred windows. One of them laughed. The driver shouted, "Are you getting on or what?"

He kept quiet, with his hands in his pockets they were suddenly enveloped, lashed by the cold. The driver said, "I'm leaving."

He started the bus. Through the blackish-brown smoke and the smell of gasoline, the two women appeared once again, as if through a curtain, one in front of the other, dressed in black, speaking to each other. The hand of one rested on the other's shoulder.

(I remember that Jeza spoke very little. He was in the habit of remaining like that, not moving, listening and, all of a sudden, he would raise his hand, stretched out, with his palm raised up. That hand erased, absorbed everything. Or both hands, with their prominent knuckles, suddenly crossed. Jeza never said very much, but the things he did say were heard. Jeza did much more than what he said. Now Jeza is nothing, scarcely even that, something startling, a surprise, hands raised from among the dead. And the dead, what is special about the dead now?)

One of the women said, "You've missed the bus."

They were looking at him. They still had their arms around each other like an unusual alliance.

"Yes."

The woman who had her hand on the other woman's shoulder, looked at him from top to bottom. Her hair was hidden under a black head-scarf tied at the back of her neck. The other woman seemed subdued, as though sleeping heavily because of the weight of friendship, of that friendly hand on her shoulder. At least so it appeared. As though one had been consoling the other for something great and terribly simple, like death.

"Did you miss it, or did you decide not to take it?"

He wanted to answer, but he could not say anything.

And the woman shrugged her shoulders and added, "I'm asking because this driver is such an animal, poor guy… that's why I'm asking you, not for any other reason."

"I let him go."

The woman nodded vaguely. Then she looked at the other woman, who remained submissive, heavily asleep against that hand. They said good-bye and then parted. The woman who had not spoken left first, with little steps like a lost little goat, huddled up, her arms crossed over her stomach. The other turned once more to look at him before going toward the bridge.

The sun had set, everything appeared wrapped up in a blue, phosphorescent cold. The white arrow pointed toward an unknown road.

(When I saw Jeza stretched out like a clod of earth, his eyes open, I thought, never again will I smile, never again will anything seem happy to me, never again on this earth will I have a taste for anything." And, nevertheless, everything has gone on as before, even before knowing him. Jeza has died. He is dead, and nothing more. We will almost never speak about him. As if he had not been born. He is dead, that's all, dead and passed on insofar as the living are concerned, those who keep on breathing every day. Laughing, weeping, being furious, being happy, being quiet. Alive and trodding on the earth kneaded by countenances and eyes and hands, like Jeza; by bones, like Jeza; by blackish, discarded toys, like Jeza; by dark and macabre holes, like Jeza. So it is, there is no reason to beat around the bush. Jeza has died, his face stuck to his bones like a crust of mud that is about to crack into pieces from one moment to the other. And the eyes so, like two pieces of glass. They are not eyes, they are not anything, not even last spring's golden and sticky leaves lying on the scorched earth. Not even that. They don't even arouse terror. Dead, and nothing more than dead.)

A throng of boys burst into the street, screaming. The first, about ten years old, had short legs and black socks.

(A coward, just a coward, letting the bus get away, getting off three, four, five—I don't know exactly how many—towns before, to not have to confront her, with her round and feverish eyes, her boy's eyes—I will never be able to think that she has a woman's eyes—in order not to have to say to her what is gnawing at me. I'll look at her, I'll come close, she'll stretch out her hand part-way. And she'll ask me, "and how about Jeza," without any words, simply with her eyes, just with gestures such as quickly brushing her hair back from her face.)

The throng of boys stopped. The boy with the black socks stood with his mouth half-opened. He was a child, just a child. Nevertheless in his features there was already a hint of the man that he would become (the sensible man he will be, strong and Godless, irreproachable, was already evident in the projection of his forehead, in his eyeballs, in his half-opened mouth covered with saliva.) He felt a quick and sterile wrath.

"What are you looking at? Get away from here!"

The child looked at his companions and raised a shoulder. He was carrying a hoop of wire, held by an iron hook. It brought him back to a time in the past, days in the past, a voice which told him to keep quiet. (Only children of isolated towns like this use these hoops. They don't use them in the cities, the children...) The boy whispered something to his companions. A timid laughter moved them quickly, crossed their little mobile mouths, a laughter impetuous and a little bit frightened, like a clearing of the throat. They got lost again, with a noise like taut ropes being struck. All of them carried hoops of thick wire held by iron hooks. They were running races. They rushed down the road, between the rows of chestnut trees, beyond the bridge. A glow seemed to accompany them now in their headlong flight. (Coward, coward, coward. That's what I am. A coward.) He turned the corner of the square.

In the street that went down toward the sawmills, he saw a cafe with wide doors. All at once the whole street had begun to smell of wood.

There were small marble tables with holes in the center. (Surely in the summer they stick hot, faded umbrellas and sunshades in them. And the sun will be like handfuls of red and ferocious dust against the front of the buildings.) There was no one at the tables. A fly, grown stiff with cold, crept blindly on the window pane, somewhere on the lower part. The waiter hit it with the napkin he carried languidly on his shoulder; the pane reverberated and the fly fell. Without enthusiasm the waiter smiled at him through the window pane. Then the waiter turned around and approached him.

"Aren't you cold?" he said to him. "Nobody sits there in this weather. There is a good fire in the stove inside."

Nobody sits here now. (They all do the same. A group says what ought to be, or can be, done. The others imitate, obey.) He went in.

The flames showed red in the opening of the stove. The waiter now seemed satisfied; he was poking in the fire with a little hook, as he opened and closed the little window of the stove. It was like a big and beautiful toy that he was very proud of. He looked at him and smiled.

"It gives off heat, huh?"

"When is another bus coming by?"

The waiter made a vague gesture.

"I saw what happened, the driver left right in your face—but that driver.... Did you let him go on purpose, or did you miss it?"

He confined himself to unwrapping the lumps of sugar. One of them bounced out of the tiny brown cup and rapidly dripped tiny stains of coffee as it melted.

"Well," said the waiter. "Another bus is leaving tomorrow morning around eleven. But it goes only as far as the junction..." The waiter said a name that did not inspire any feeling in him, that brought nothing to his memory.

"Then, there's only one in the evening. I mean, yours; you already know about that one."

The coffee, watery and with too much sugar, grew cold at the bottom of the cup.

"It's good," the waiter said with a slight wink. In that wink there was submission, modest happiness, perplexity, admiration. "The coffee's good. The owner bought a very good machine. I believe it's the best one around here." Manuel smiled at him faintly, and paid. The waiter bent over the money and immediately his smile disappeared. There was no tip.

"Do you know where I can spend the night?"

"We have rooms here." Once more the smile broke out, full of hope.

A strong smell of bleach and the maid's outrageously loud song woke him up. The sun was coming in through the blinds. He hadn't closed the shutters. He was thirsty. He immediately looked at his watch for fear that the night time had gone by. But he remembered immediately. The eleven o'clock bus didn't go any further than the junction. As if his thoughts had begun to scream, like the voice of the girl scrubbing the landing, there, just behind the door, the waiter knocked and said, "Listen, if you wish, there is a car going there."

"When?" His heart began to throb dully, like an old and out-of-tune motor. "Now, in twenty minutes, they say."

There was a chipped porcelain washstand and a pitcher. With a shudder he poured the pitcher of water over his head and the back of his neck.

When he came out onto the landing, his ears were burning. The waiter asked him, "Coffee?" hoping to use the machine again. On the landing an old wall-clock showed ten thirty. He looked at his watch again with astonishment. On the small face of his watch the hands showed sixteen minutes after seven.

"Don't pay attention, it's stopped," laughed the waiter, as he disappeared down the staircase toward the coffee maker, full of ineffable pleasure. His hands manoeuvered the machine with a feverish voluptuousness. A noisy, hot steam blurred the surface of the metal. With a dreary smile he served a little cup, holding the saucer with both hands.

"Good, good," the waiter said, looking at him, rubbing his hands. "And look, they told me one is leaving in that direction; and I said to myself: I'm going to alert the young man who was here yesterday, the one who missed the bus."

He took a sip. Two men, wrapped in their overcoats, were crossing the cold street; a little cloud of steam was coming out of their mouths. At the corner of the square, on two rough little wooden doors painted yellow, had been written: MEN AND WOMEN in red letters. From beneath the doors, dampness and a strong smell of ammonia overflowed.

"It's a taxi, said the waiter, walking ahead of him. In the pale morning light his jacket had the yellow color of old tablecloths kept in a linen closet. "Look, he had two customers get off and he had a seat left for you."

He felt an unexpected uneasiness, as if the slight smile which floated around the waiter would fall to the ground, around them both, like a rain of sand. He felt miserable. (He was going to tell her, "Don't you think anything more about him, don't ever expect any news of him. You have to know it, once and for all, he's dead.")

2

Marcela would say:

"Don't open the window."

But Marta would open it, because if she didn't, she felt she would suffocate. Marcela had just lit the wood in the small corner fireplace.

"I'm telling you, why light the fire if you stand there in front of the window? You'll never get well that way."

What she liked best about Marcela was precisely that she never beat around the bush. She always told the truth, or what she believed to be the truth. Pity was something else. At the beginning (many months ago, it seemed impossible) she had said to her, "Girl, you don't look well, not well at all." She had said it to her like that, standing in front of her, well planted on the ground they were standing on. And she didn't feel fear when she heard her; rather, an unusual feeling of security. There, at least, was someone who didn't go in for flattery, didn't lie. Yes, pity was something else and Marcela had it in its truest sense.

"These shitty little houses," Marcela now said, with a certain panting in her voice because of her bent over-posture. "The only good thing about them is that they get warm in a second. The walls are still damp. Still, it's not like the other, where lately the wind was already coming in through cracks. It wasn't a house, it was a sieve."

The child was crying.

"There it is," Marcela said. And her face filled with brightness. It was not only the reflection of the flames, it was her own brightness, that sometimes came up to her own eyes (full, it seems, of all the fears and suffering of the world) and, nevertheless, as though bathed suddenly by a light, just like a wave (unexpectedly, one never knew when). She looked at Marcela with the limitless admiration she felt for her in those moments. An admiration and a candor that curtailed all words, including all thoughts. Suddenly, Marcela could be the whole world, with its trees, rivers, mountains and roads. All the superficial things she had read or learned, her studies, fled like superficial birds of men's thoughts.

"Well, really, don't you hear your son?" Marcela scolded.

Marta scowled and ran, like a sleepwalker, to the next room. She opened the shutters and saw the child seated between the wrinkled blankets. He was congested from crying and his eyes were red from weeping. She took him in her arms. His body was warm. She rested his head covered with shining blond hair against her shoulder. He began to hiccup softly. She quietly put her hand on the back of his neck—she wanted to pacify it, subdue it, the way Marcela's hand did. But her hand was too quick, she didn't know how to do it. Only Marcela could do these things. The child changed his hiccup to a special kind of purring, almost like a little song. She pushed away his head and looked at him. (Almost two. Two years of breathing, of looking with that pair of damp plums, of hazelnut color, of smelling the earth, the logs, the smoke, the trees, the nettles burning from the sun. The white walls under the sun. Almost two years of searching blindly, unknowingly, the reason for being. The white walls under the sun. The reason for all things....)

"Don't cry," she said.

"Yes, he died," Manual said for the second time, as though obsessed.

She had heard. Nevertheless she kept on there, in front of him, with the child hanging from her neck. A picture of womanhood, shown for centuries and centuries in paintings, murals, windows, plates, sculptures, photography, and etchings. The picture of a woman, although she didn't appear to be so... perhaps because of those eyes that he had never wanted to confront...those amazing eyes, incredulous, a little girl's eyes.

"Sit down," he said.

He offered her the chair, but she did not move. Marcela appeared in the door, looking at him wildly.

"Brute!"

Manuel sat down, trembling, in the chair he had offered her. Trembling, not because he knew it, but because he saw it, his two slow, stupid hands, trembling in front of his eyes.

"You are a brute," Marcela added, aside. "Only brutes say things like that."

A touch of white froth appeared on the lips of the country woman (of the farm worker enraged when faced with destructive wild animals. I remember how once I saw a country woman cut a baby fox in two, with her sickle.)

The child began to laugh, pointing at Marcela with his chubby hand. Perhaps he found it funny to see her angry. (Enraged by Jeza's death. Jeza is the father of this child and this child will never know, will never live through this death, as we are living through, in agony, for months. Never. He will grow up and they will say to him, "Your father died." And he will know of that death, he will hear of that death, but he will never experience that death, as I am experiencing it at this moment. As she is realizing it herself, now, in this moment.)

"Be quiet," the woman said.

Her voice sounded unusual. It was very strange to hear her voice at that moment when the logs were exploding in the fireplace. With little cracks, scattering a tenuous hiss of burning gas and a weak and irritating odor. Marcela collapsed in a chair, resting her forehead on her arm—a robust and dark arm, with her sleeves rolled up to her arms—and cried silently. It was her cold, depersonalized voice that made her cry in an almost mechanical way.

The driver appeared in the doorway. His hands were stained with black grease and he was rubbing them with a rag.

"Are you going, or staying here?" he asked.

He was a chubby, hairy man. At that moment he realized that he hadn't spoken to him during the entire trip.

"Wait for me," he said. "Go have a drink…wait, I haven't decided."

The driver cast a glance at the two women and his eyes opened a little. He gestured vaguely, saying,

"Don't rush, there's no hurry."

He went out and saw the humid brilliance of his little eyes. (Dealers everywhere. I feel weary. Logical, solid, natural dealers. The waiter with the saucer between his hands, smiling at me. The driver making things easy. All of them seated patiently at the door of their shops, waiting. Waiting for me. Fanning away the sweat. Fat, wise, useful dealers. Fanning themselves at the door of hunger, of desire, smiling, waiting. That's what life is, a chubby and patient dealer, sitting at the door of his shop, of his little shop, waiting, with a sour and contained brilliance in his eyes. I am well acquainted with this image. Life is this image. Only death, like Jeza, has great serenity, sumptuous silence. Death, death, death. I am now completely forsaken, the way I have never felt in my solitary life. An unusual forsakenness that doesn't desire signs of affection or human solidarity, that doesn't desire the closeness of men, that doesn't ask for anything on earth. I am terrified, frightened by this thought. Death left me feeling alone. Only death is my ally, it could be my death, and it has left me alone. When Jeza was alive I already vaguely felt this. And now Jeza has snatched everything from me, has left me without death, only with life, with that kind of life without reason and without convictions, linking together minutes and seconds. Only Jeza knew, only Jeza was sure; and he carried off with him, with his unmovable security, the total security of death, my great reason.)

An incredible sun came out from behind the mist. It lit up the walls, the wooden table, the ceramic pots she had so lovingly sought out and classified (with her eyes of a boy who is still discovering the immense treasures of the earth). Everything was filled with light, almost without transition. But it is a light of blackness, like a flash of lightning that, in a second, turns everything to day, but a day incrusted in the night. And scarcely has the flash of lightning disappeared than the night still exists and floods over us, weighs upon us, invades us like a sea. It is like repeating a piece of one's life. He straddled the chair, the same one he had offered her. He felt like he was a spectator of himself, with his arms hanging down like pendulums, trembling. Once more, once more the same story.

(The house was on the slope like a cube of whitewash, the garden dark and luminous, the buzzing of bees, and the mortifying smell of the flowers confounding one's reason. And my mother was in front of me, silent, trembling, looking at me with her blue eyes like mirrors in which the sea was always reflected. And also between us there was a subtle thread which united us more than all words. In the boat was the body of Jose Taronji. "My father's body," I forced myself to say, beating words into my temples as a savage furiously and stubbornly beats a piece of leather. But the name of another lay between the thread which united us, mother and me, a murderer through omission, through indifference, through contempt, through selfishness. The name of the worst of the murderers, whom I loved, even then.)

"Excuse me," he said.

She leaned against the wall. The sun now threw off flames from her hair. In the roots, in the clean and straight part that divided her hair in two, the blond was almost white, shining. Then it turned a golden color, slowly, as if it were dying (as all of her, a flame which is born rebellious and goes out, dies down).

"When was it?" she finally asked.

(Just like my mother would ask, "When son?" And I said to her, "A short while ago. Apparently he tried to escape….I found him on the beach at Santa Catalina, next to an abandoned boat"…And, at that moment, as now, I'm useless, I'm a hindrance, like all things and all beings for her. And I don't even know, as Jeza knew. Because of that he's dead; and I, on the other hand, who is nothing and does nothing, keep on living.)

He said, "I went to see him yesterday, they hadn't told me anything…They made me wait, and then they gave me a package with his things. I don't know if you… I don't know whether you'll want to keep it."

"Did you see him?"

"Yes."

Stupidly, he repeated it twice. She returned his same frightened look. Nothing more.

Then she turned halfway around and went to the door. Over her shoulder she looked at the child's head (the two of them have the same eyes). Marcela raised her head. Tears were shining, caught in the lines around her mouth. She said, "I'm going to tell you something, Manuelito."

(How it surprises me now, that diminutive. When women like Marcela call men by their boyhood names, something is going on, something moving or exasperating.)

"I'm going to tell you something," she repeated. She had taken a knife from the top of the table and had begun to scrape the edge without going so far as cutting it; that act had a threat of something cruel and prudent, more than a scream.

"Cursed be the person guilty of Jeza's death. And may God not have pity on him."

At that moment there was no hate in Marcela's eyes. Only a quiet, passive mourning. (As though coming from the depths of the water, as when I bent over the wall and heard the echo of the silence.)

"He was like a brother to you," Manuel said, almost without realizing it. She interrupted him with a brusque movement of her head.

"He was my brother. My brother, do you hear? More than

Simeón and Zacarias were. Jeza was my brother."

(Brothers, my brothers, where are you? I was looking for you and you were ciphers, beautiful names, voices that were calling and I didn't hear. My brothers. Brothers, don't you remember how I wanted to go down to your garden? My brothers, I am guilty of everything. Everyone accuses me of being guilty, because betrayal is a part of me, like my weight. As a child I wanted love. Afterward I discovered that it was not love, because they taught me love there, where love is yet another cipher, and I said to myself "It is not love that must be parcelled out, as one distributes the seed of the fields." Neither reasons, nor words, Jeza was a living fact, a fact, not a cipher, not a word, not a forest of words where men search in vain for brothers. And that woman who says, "He was my brother," even though the lost blood of Jeza does not run in her veins, knows more than I do about things that have to do with men. Only now does hatred come to me. Hatred without passion for everyone who deformed my life. For everyone who said to me, "Come with me, you are the king of my house," and forced me to say, "No, I belong to my brothers." And my brothers did not take me in.)

3

It's strange that I'm here, in front of our son. It's strange that he's our son, and that he's called Alejandro. It's all very strange, this house, this woman called Marcela, who believes she's Jeza's sister, that boy called Manuel who speaks to me as though we were something, one to the other. I mean, it's unusual for someone to believe that he has some connection with me, friendship, sympathy, simple acquaintanceship. I don't know anyone. I don't know anything about anything. Jeza was the only one I knew. I would like to know where Jeza is and why Jeza doesn't die. Jeza isn't dying because I am here, standing, and I am looking at Alejandro's eyes, which are also looking at me. I see his eyes shine and his nose is a crushed stain, with two pink, little holes. Alejandro is Jeza's son, but it doesn't seem to me that he has any connection with him. It's very strange, everything is very strange. But I belong much more to Jeza than does his child. I, my body, my hair, my teeth, my eyes, my skin have gotten more from Jeza than this child who is his son. There is much more of Jeza in me than this child. I have to take care of myself, then, to feed the Jeza who is inside me. No, all this is useless, all this is empty and stupid. The pain has not yet reached me. I am astonished, yes, very astonished, my twenty years weighing on me, the death of Jeza weighing on top of those twenty years. So then I've been growing and renewing myself for twenty-two years, to get ready for Jeza's death. This child doesn't have much connection with us. It's something that weighs down more than the body, more than blood. I don't know what his name is, nor who he is. I chose Jeza and he accepted me. That's all there is to it. Nobody chose this child. But I don't want to live, spied on by memories. With memories always weighing on one's shoulder. No, that can't be. I want to get rid of all that. Like Jeza used to do. If things were the opposite, he would not have done it this way. Definitely, for me there is no other duty on earth than this, to forget what I ought to forget and go forward. We'll arrive somewhere. Ourselves, our children, or our grandchildren. It would be a great effort on my part to forget Jeza, taking into account that I ought not to forget what he said, what he did. Because Jeza was present, now, forever, in everything I might do. Also in Manuel. Perhaps he had to die so that we might begin to understand him. Including Marcela. Marcela who

when she feared for him said, "That one is as stubborn as a mule."
Even she will now begin to understand something about him. In
reality he was surrounded by blind men, by dubious characters, or by
an unknown faithfulness that could not give satisfaction. My faithfulness could not give him satisfaction. Jeza used to say to me, "I want
you to understand the reason for all this. I don't want you to do it for
my sake, or because you think it's a good thing. I want you to know
why it seems a good thing to you." I didn't understand him. Only now,
in this darkness, in this awful silence that begins to surround and
negate all things, do I believe that I am beginning to understand his
words and his actions. Jeza, Jeza, where are you now? You are a fact,
complete and closed off, a fact that weighs upon us. You used to say
very little. Jeza, you spoke very little. There is no one more real now
than you are. You have been something, something which happened,
certainly, which has happened. Not us, who will pass like something
that was wished for, explained, written. Jeza, you are something that
has happened, that is still happening, Jeza, in me, in Manuel, in all the
others on earth. Jeza, Jeza, I have learned nothing about you, even
now. Now that you are dead we will begin to understand you. How
easy it can be perhaps. I wonder if that would make you glad. But few
things made you glad, things that were always unexplainable, rain,
bread. Marcela used to say, "He is easy to satisfy, poor guy. Everybody knows that he is always boiling inside about other things." And,
nevertheless, nothing seemed purer than you. We were all around you,
like a jumbled mass of thorns, of rotted desires, of rotted hopes. You
were like a tree, you had to be, you were. We wanted to be, Jeza. We
wish, really wish to be, Jeza. A tree doesn't die. That's what you are.
What does Manuel mean when he says, "Jeza has died?" I have never
heard anything more stupid. It's as though one were to say "You
know, that tree has died." It's the same thing. I have to understand this
very well, neither words, nor false concepts, nor conventional reasons. The one thing that is certain is that which happens. Jeza is
something that happens, that is there. At that moment the child cried,
he was struggling to get out of her arms. She realized it because
Marcela took him from her arms and put a hand on her shoulder.
Marcela said, "Come now, girl, come now."

But she shook her head negatively. She looked at the door, the
picture of light through which Marcela had left taking the child by the

hand. Her heavy legs didn't make a noise. She heard footsteps, slow and creaking. They were the footsteps of someone who was uncertain, who hesitated, forsaken. Manuel was very strange. He appeared to be much more deprived by Jeza's absence than she. And suddenly, like a blow, something broke the cold. (Something bends the high branches that shake inside me, the way the apple tree used to shake. Something similar to rain, atrocious, devastating, brutal, because it's not there. Absence. Manuel is more deprived by Jeza's absence. Absence is this. I will never see Jeza again. No, I'll never see Jeza again. I'll never see Jeza anymore. I'll not see his eyes. I'll not see his hands again. I'll never see Jeza. Alejandro will never see Jeza, nobody will ever see Jeza. How is it possible that no one will see Jeza? How is it possible that, against all my strength, against all my reason and determination that this be so profound and so damaging. Of what accursed kind is this our flesh that makes it so monstrous, so unbearable not to see someone? From what miserable root did my eyes grow, so that not seeing Jeza could be so cruel, so desolating? I say to myself, yes, that I ought not to remember; because to remember is sand between the fingers, dry and empty sand, that does not bear fruit. But I know, I remember, I experience not seeing. Jeza grew close to me and, suddenly, in the middle of the light, I pictured him. My eyes pictured him, in front of me, grain by grain of light. I'll never see Jeza, never again will I see Jeza.)

Everything broke, opened up into two. And she remembered Marcela, how her powerful farm-woman hands seized the suspicious fruit between her hands and, without the help of a knife, split it open, saw the creaking tearing of the flesh, indented in two; and Marcela's voice which said, "It's rotten, you see? So wholesome on the outside and worm-eaten on the inside." Now everything was being broken, was splitting between bestial hands against which reason, judgement could do nothing. Reason was worm-eaten, it was wholesome on the outside, glossy, pure and simple reason, only on the skin. Man grows from some ignoble material which, upon splitting in two, the flesh appears bitten, consumed, gnawed by a dark worm). She did not have tears, not a single one flowed from her. And, nevertheless, through that interior fire, through that shaking that she could not control, she cried mutely, with dry eyes.

4

"What are you going to do now?" Manuel asked.

They were seated, one in front of the other. Between them was the table that Marcela had scraped with the knife, as if she had wanted to erase all the corruption of the world. She continued to look at him, deliberate, almost inhuman.

"But I don't know....I don't know what I can do for you. Tell me and I'll do it. The fact is, I know so little about you. I have almost never seen you before."

Unexpectedly she spoke.

"How did you start writing to me?"

"You see, I went to the Port. In those days I really needed to return. Es Mariné gave me Jacobo's address and told me, 'Jeza is in jail and she is in a town out in the country with the sister of Zacarias and Simeón.' Then I began to go to the jail to see him. I was afraid that they would make it difficult, but... you know, my situation has changed recently. Before now I was denied everything; now I'm a person with privileges. Now I'm allowed everything or almost everything. Then I began to send letters to Marcela. I knew that she would give them to you."

"I never thanked you, but your letters were the only good thing that has happened lately. I wasn't able to see him or write to him. Thanks, Manuel."

"Don't say that," his voice sounded brusque and (ah! old Sanamo: You have become very brusque, Manuel). He felt a physical, intolerable pain, right there in the jugular (so vulnerable to death).

"You probably heard things about me," she said.

Like something that had been suppressed for a long time, her voice rose, with the surprise of water, fire, suddenly purifying the indifferent earth of men.

"I suppose so," she added. "I wasn't well thought of in those regions. Not even by Jeza's friends. Nobody wanted me, they had their reasons. I wasn't to be trusted. They were right."

"It doesn't matter to me," he said, passionately. "It doesn't matter a bit to me what they say. I knew that you were his wife. That was enough. You know, for me Jeza has been transformed into the only bearable thing. Especially now that he is dead. The rest can't move me too much, the world keeps on being an alienated thing for me. Only Jeza was able to let me predict anything. I beg of you that..."

She became silent, intimidated. She looked at him in a new way, surprised and almost monstrously happy.

"Tell me," she said, almost voicelessly.

Unexpectedly they had begun to whisper (as if a thousand ears, as if monstrous and malign snails placed on the earth all around us, were opening up).

"What was he for you? Why has he changed so much for others...? You know, Manuel, there is something I can't understand. Jeza was something unattainable, he was something all of us wanted, but, at times, I think...it seems as if we had invented him. You tell me now that you saw him and I wonder if someone had seen him on some occasion, or whether only we carry him inside, like a desire."

"I have seen him," he said firmly. "I spoke with him about eleven times. There were two gratings and a man between the two of us listening to all that we said. But I saw him there and that was enough for me. Then I would write to you."

(The pale man said, "Well, it is not necessary any more." He gave me back the tobacco, the chocolate, those childish things that at times can mean so much. Then he said to me, "Sit down outside there, your friend is going to send regards." And he brought me the very soft wind that I knew so well. But why am I going to tell that to her, with her round, thirsty eyes? And, "I can imagine it now, when? You arrive at the right moment, this early morning hour," I said, "Can I see him?" And I put the money in his hand that was already waiting for it—like a soft and damp jawbone. He said, "You can ask the director." The son of Jorge de Son Major—not the poor and nauseating Manuel Taronji, in whose well they threw a dead dog—saw him. He was there, tense, earthy, he with his noble skull stretching his delicate skin and his blue eyes open to the void).

"Manuel," she said. And she gave him her hand and he squeezed it.

(I feel a desire for words, words that always appeared insufficient to me. You can tell me everything you want. Whatever you might not want to tell, I will not listen to. But tell me something that can do us a lot of good.)

She added:

"They spoke ill of me to you, isn't that true? Including Jacobo, he included spoke ill of me too, didn't he?"

"Yes," he answered with a contradictory relief.

"I like it when you tell the truth. I'm tired of keeping quiet, I'm offended by so much silence." She looked around, at the quiet hills, the earth, the haziness of things (moments rolled opaquely at the end of time).

"Come with me," Manuel said. "Come, we'll talk. Leave all this, it oppresses me to see it. My house is near the sea, you can go there if you want. And we'll talk. I don't know why, it seems to me that we are able to talk a lot about everything that has to do with us. I suspect that something is not lost."

Suddenly she appeared much younger than he, in spite of the fact that she was three years older. She appeared lost and frightened.

"Come, leave that."

"Yes," she said in a whisper. "Let's get away from here. I have been silent for so long that I almost don't recognize my own voice. Manuel, let me say certain things to you, perhaps stupid and useless things, but if I speak to you, little by little, their sense will emerge...don't I know how to say it, Manuel?"

"Yes. Yes, you know how."

She stroked his cheek with the back of her hand. It was an almost mechanical gesture, but more comforting than all the words of friendship that she was capable of saying.

The driver looked in again, impatiently.

"Have you made up your mind?" He looked at her and she scarcely hesitated an instant.

"Yes, we're going back immediately. Just give me time to pack my suitcase and we'll leave."

Marcela came in slowly.

"It's the best thing you can do," she said. "Try to recover his body if you can. Go with Manuel; don't worry about the child. I'll take care of him meanwhile. But stop off there, ask for his body, ask that they allow you to bury it."

Everyone stopped in front of the rail fence, as she now did, with a kind of stupor, of a strange expectation. The silence and the murmuring of the sea, the long cry of the wind on the cliff detained them before crossing the threshold.

"Is this your house?"

"Now it is. You can stay here all the time you want, nobody will bother you. I live there, down the cliff."

"Nobody bothers me," she said with her almost overflowing apathy.

He pushed her gently by the shoulder and they went in.

Sanamo arrived, huddling in his jacket. (A long, somber, shady loggia, the sinister white of the arches sheltered a heavy silence.) The shutters, painted blue, appeared hermetically closed. The lavender heads of the flowers were already dead; and the closed woven vine was losing its leaves, uncovering its delicate black skeleton, with a thousand arms stretched out toward the walls, like a mute and desperate supplication. The magnolias were there. In this month, bare. The reddish tile roof, the tiles so neatly matched up, the whiteness of the whitewash; and everything so old, so ruinously loved.

Sanamo lit small bonfires with the dead leaves. A reddish smoke floated among the trees of the garden. The smell of the burning leaves got in her nose, like a drug, (no flowers remained, only the despised roses of October, blood red, almost black; like malicious countenances lying in ambush, passionately glossy and ancient, from the depths of the garden.) On the wooden table under the trees where he had been in the habit of eating, throbbed an obscure absence (and the birds, stiff with cold, came down in search of crumbs; of a presence which is no longer, nor will ever be. No one will inherit his burning afternoons, old sun, nobody will inherit his memories or the troubled sadness of his dead nights, everything has ended in muffled funeral laments and in the opaque silence of the earth, by shovelfuls on his closed, blocked up, human head. Sanamo remained with his mouth open. (He probably thought, "But that's too much, bringing home that worthless woman.")

"Open the doors, Sanamo. I don't have the keys."

The smoke came toward them in a gust of air. Beyond the walls the sea was throwing itself against the cliff. (The same sea, beating against the same walls.)

"There used to be a vine here, with grapes," Manuel said, as he guided her. "From the top of the pergola hung bunches of grapes, green and pink."

"It's their month," Sanamo said with a burning rancor in his voice. "The month of grapes, wine, roses. Everything that he loved so much."

She appeared not to hear him. She kept looking upward, her hair brilliant and golden on her shoulder, and her mouth half-opened. He then perceived the poverty of her clothes. She was wearing a sailor's turtleneck sweater, faded from many washings. Once more Sanamo drew away. He gathered the leaves with a rake. In a contained rage, he scraped the ground as if he wanted to rip across the skin of the world. In a corner of the garden, flames were crackling, lifting up gold and blue tongues. A cloud of black particles, like minute devils, fell upon the leaves, and seemed to awaken the girl. She shook her head, her shoulders.

"You never left the island?" she said suddenly.

"Never."

The rake continued piling up leaves. Sanamo placed a bunch of keys on the table. Then he left them.

5

He stopped in front of the faithful reproduction of the Delfin enclosed in a bottle.

"Es Mariné made it," Manuel explained. But he knew that she was looking without seeing, that her thoughts were lost in some place far from there.

"I don't want his body," she said suddenly. "Men have nothing to do with his corpse."

He put his hand on her shoulder and, in turn, she raised hers, small, thin and cold, and squeezed his hand.

"You never managed to see him?"

"Never after they took him away."

I wasn't even able to say goodbye to him. I hadn't seen him for 48 hours. We were summoned the same evening he had gotten together with Jacobo and the Italian sailor. I wasn't even able to say to him, "Good-bye, Jeza, good luck." Nor look at him for the last time.

His eyelids were half-closed.

"No, I didn't get to look at him for the last time; because the last day I saw him, I assure you I didn't suspect anything. I would be lying if I told you I foresaw it. It was then, in those forty-eight hours, that it came to me like an unfavorable wind. Until Jacobo telephoned me."

(Suddenly it stopped raining. For only a few minutes—it seemed—she had been hearing the beating of the water against the skylight. Without more ado, she raised her head and noticed a sticky silence like a vapor. Her head ached; she put it between her hands. It was an unusual sensation, as if that head of hers were floating in the great silence that, unexpectedly, had risen about her. She drew closer to the glass door and opened it. A whiff of fresh air entered. She saw how the drops were trembling and falling from the leaves, shining. Up there the sky was grey, swollen and lashed at like a canvas awning. She went down the little staircase and began to look for something to eat. She found a chocolate bar. She bit into it. It was earthy, with an unusual taste of a thousand things, she was not sure of what. At that moment the telephone rang and her heart skipped a beat. She felt the earthy chocolate between her teeth, as though it were sand, and stretched out her hand toward the receiver.

"Yes," she said timidly.

From the other end came the suffocated voice of Jacobo.

"Come immediately. You must come. Be careful."

She swallowed slowly, noticing her dry, clammy mouth and a horrible need to spit. Her stomach felt as though it was turning upside down. She was at the point of crying, of screaming like a rat, and shouting, "They have come. It is true that they have come. Is everything already over with, finally? "At some moment during the last 48 hours she had thought to herself *to know that everything has failed, is over with, will perhaps be a relief*. But she saw no peace, no comfort. She hung up the phone and remained silent, fearful, with her back pressed to the wall. A thought passed through her. I'm not going to move from here, even though they want that. They should come and get me. I'm not going to move from here…she knew that they were not able to come immediately, that—at the least—they would delay for eight or 10 hours…. Could she stand that condition, even for one more hour? She felt like beating her aching head against the wall, because suddenly everything seemed dull to her, everything appeared to have been carried out without skill, without precaution or care. Neither Jeza nor she nor Jacobo. Idiots confident of their lucky star. And there was no star there.)

She went toward the divan upholstered in a fabric of birds and flowers from a distant land that he had so much admired when he was a child. She sat down, distracted, and he went to get the glasses.

"Would you like a drink?"

"All right," she said.

How alone he saw her there, suddenly, and how young. Almost a girl in spite of her twenty-two years, despite all that he knew or had heard about her. Not even Es Mariné or Zacarias had liked her. ("How unfortunate, Jeza, to burden oneself with a worthless woman like that," Jose Taronji had said.) And, nevertheless, she was there, with her innocent eyes, like a small trapped fish, in the world's wide net. There was something distant, almost timeless, in her. (Certainly she is pretty.) The blond hair, smooth and soft, shone in the twilight. (But it is not her beauty that attracts him. It is something that floats in her, wherever she goes. When she speaks, when she is silent, something is alive around her; flocks of birds that cannot be seized, breaking their flight. He filled the glass and handed it to her. She drank with an almost childish relish.

"I'm afraid," she said unexpectedly.

How often he had heard that word.

"Of what?"

"Of myself, now that he isn't here. I don't have confidence in myself. I'm afraid of wandering about and betraying him."

They looked at each other in silence.

"Then how insignificant we are," said Manuel in a whisper.

She leaned her head against the back of the chair. Big yellow and blue birds were beating their wings, immobile, arrested in a strange flight, on the upholstery around her head.

"What a short and ugly life," she said. "It can be told in a few not very edifying words."

He brought up the big Turkish cushion (as Sanamo used to say, "Do you know the story of the prince threatened by death, the one with the silver turban? His father wanted to save him from death, so he he locked him up and cared for him. He had a grotto dug for him under the rock and only went to see him and bring him fruit. And one day, cutting a piece of melon, sweet as honey, he left his dagger in a high crevice in the grotto. And the dagger fell on the son while he was sleeping and severed his heart." And I too was locked up, in order that life might not contaminate me. But life and death find a way through fissures and seams, life and death break out and cleave the heart.) He had to make an effort to follow what she was saying.

"My mother had a hotel in San Juan. That was around 1933 or 34. But before that she had a secondhand store and a pawn shop."

(Her hand stretched out, her fingernails long. She dreamed at night about her mother's angry and harsh eyes, the burning globes of her enormous eyes, her faded beauty. She knew how to root through poverty and how to gain by it. She remembered the secondhand store in Madrid, in a little side street in the Corredera Baja. The sheets examined by hand, the children's overcoats carefully checked from the lining to the lapels, the collars which her fingers scraped in search of a stain.

"One duro for this."

The silver place-settings, the packages lined up on the shelves; that porcelain shepherdess in the hands of the old lady with the powdered hair, whose voice shook when she said, "This is the last thing I have left." Her mother took it. And she notices the pain in the eyes of the old woman, from whose neck hung a gold chain, with a dead portrait—photographs die too—as dead as her faded splendor. Her mother said, "We can't have sentimentalism here, *señora*. The business would fail."

And, when the old woman had gone and the doorbell had rung above her powdered hair, her mother's teeth shone and she said, "It's very nice to go around begging for a little compassion and romanticism when you have squandered a fortune, a real fortune in luxuries and automobiles and gigolos."

"What's a gigolo?"

"Get back to work, child."

The faithful and troubled Dionisia who, at that time, had not yet turned grey and who wore a black braid around her head, as blue as her mustache, said, "Elena, you ought to put her in a full-time boarding school. She's getting older and it's not proper that she hear and see so many things."

Her mother looked at her with an uneasy curiosity.

"Older?" she said. And it was the first time that she noticed the alarm in her big eyes. She said, "Very well. I'll think about it soon."

At that time, she was going to a modest, private neighborhood high-school near the shop. She did her homework in the shop, on the very counter, near the enormous iron clock full of dust that they would never sell. Winter set in, with the pale sun raising up a sharp odor of wood and dust in the packages lined up on the shelves with their names and dates, where children's and men's overcoats, wedding rings, antique clocks, fans, lacquer boxes, bracelets and sheets from a bride's trousseau slept. The porcelain shepherdess was there, above the counter, terribly frightened. She stretched out her hand timidly toward the shepherdess, and Dionisia, Mama's friend and partner, gave her a cuff.

"Don't do that, stupid. You could break it."

The shepherdess was wrapped up in tissue paper, carefully kept in a little cardboard box and classified with the name of the old lady and the date of her pawn.

"The hotel was her pride, her passion, all the she had built up with effort. She managed to keep hiding me until I was eighteen."

"Why?" (What has been imprisoned tries to break out, break its glass prison, throw itself like a meteor, toward some place where it can not hear the old women nor the forgotten lost confessions of children.)

"She kept me practically locked up. She didn't want anyone to know that she had such a grown-up daughter. She kept me in boarding school as much as possible. Other girls left at seventeen, but I didn't. I remained the maximum amount of time. She would have muzzled me, locked me up, if she had been able to, so that no one should ever see me. Perhaps she hated me.

"Why?"

Because she wanted to keep hold of a man much younger than she. She was mad about him, she was afraid that he would find out about my age. His name was Raul. For her it was a sickness, a real sickness. I had to pay for that desperate love of hers."

(It was not a sea like that of the island, a sea engulfed in a strange silence, as though a storm kept within it might rise up. It was a grey and exasperating sea and she ran about on the beach, picking up pink shells to make herself a necklace. The hotel rose up, beautiful and ruinous, like its owner, near the wall. Her mother had said, "Don't come close to the hotel until four," and so she hung around. She was fifteen and her mother had just met Raul. It was vacation time. High up in the hotel were narrow rooms for servants. They put her up there, with her dolls and her bicycle.

"You're going to live very well here, isn't that true, sweetie?"

Dionisia, now the housekeeper, with a blue mustache above her lip (—the little girl saw how she covered it with white paste at night), left her for a while and sat down near the open window, fanning herself with a paper fan that had an advertisement for cookies on it—she asked Dionisia, "Why are you doing that, Dionisia? Shut up, idiot." She shoved her into her little bed.

"Now go to sleep at once, and don't even think about coming downstairs."

"My mother worked a great deal all her life and finally she had that hotel. Many foreigners and Spaniards used to come during the summertime. But the roulette game was always open."

For the first time Manuel saw her smile.

"I had to do everything, including eating, on the sly. I had to be hidden from everyone, from the customers and especially from Raul. She spoke about me; she used to say to him, "The girl, my little daughter..." but she always managed so that no one would ever see me. It humiliated me a great deal when they forced me to dress like a child, to do my hair in braids like a girl. But I admit that my mother was a very unfortunate woman. Now I understand, afterward, how unfortunate she must have felt to be able to do that. She feared, trembled, each moment that passed, as if she were saying to herself, "One minute less, one instant more of old age, one moment more of Marta's growing up."

"Your name is Marta?"

"Yes. You didn't know?"

"No. Jose Taronji, Jacobo, and the others used to call you Jeza's wife. Now I realize that. I didn't know what your name was. I used to send the letters to Marcela, remember?"

6

"You have paid for a crime you didn't commit. Marcela told me so. They're going to make him into a real saint. But I believe in an order of things that has to arrive one day."

There was a pain and a restrained desperation in his words.

She took a sip and a thin radiance appeared on her cheekbones.

"I never had a childhood, Manuel. You did. My childhood is something dry and dead. I remember that as a reward I wanted to be like my mother, only that I hated her and I admired her. I was so much alone, with her and with a horrible woman called Dionisia that only knew how to say "her," referring to my mother. I was fed up already when I did something. Fed up and tired of being alone. I had to avenge myself."

"What did you do?"

Suddenly a great tenderness overcame him, through her dryness, in her lost voice, like a bird. (Together the broken pieces of that which is not childhood, reconstruct them and leave them in some place in order to be able to touch it one day, like a rare object.) Manuel refilled the glasses. Sanamo kept on lighting the bonfires in the garden. It smelled of smoke. He repeated the question in a voice that was, in spite of himself, overbearing.

"What did you do?"

He was looking toward the large windows with their drawn back velvet curtains. Formerly there were no doves here, only a conservatory, cold, empty of life like a desert. At one time it could have appeared pink and familiar to him, but now he imagined it to be a prison, between the high stone walls.

The wine shone on Marta's lips and there was something deep red in her radiance, in spite of her paleness. He found her to be distant, like someone one had heard about at some time, something they had told him about and which he could—in spite of himself even by examining photographs or documents—believe.

"I wasn't a child," she said, like a scream.

At that moment he realized the primitive beauty of her eyes, of the unbound force that filled those golden eyes, which seemed to him those of an innocent child.

(Elena, her mother, was a beautiful woman; or, at least, she seemed so to her. Tall, with long legs and big hands, possessed of an individual beauty, with fingernails that curved down like those of a bird. When she was newly made-up, Marta was forced to study her for a few seconds, with a certain dread, and to decide she is beautiful. But when she went downstairs to say good morning to her and found her in front of her dressing table, just having gotten up out of bed, with her cup of coffee getting cold, sitting as though bewildered in front of jars, tubes and bottles, when she saw the thousands and thousands of tiny gashes around her eyes and mouth, in the furrows and the space between the eyebrows, the livid bags under her eyes, the almost animal stupor in her pupils, the center of the pupils dilated and phosphorescent, then she thought, "She's worse than ugly, ugliness was never so horrible as she is, now, in the harsh light of day."

Upstairs there, under the roof, in the long, narrow room, Elena had lined up a dozen dolls. She had never liked dolls, and these gave an effect of horror during the night, when the green and red bolts of lightning would appear on the dolls at night from the electric sign of the Casa de los Negros, and the flashing sign, yellow and green, that would advertise cigarettes on the flat roof terrace of the house across from her window. The horrible and chubby cheeked dolls, dressed in real silk, with their yellow and pink wigs like rough and shiny burlap, and their perfume—Elena would come in with her atomizer whenever a mad euphoria possessed her. She would come upstairs laughing and cover her and the dolls with perfume, while Dionisia looked on with opaque and swollen eyes in her withered face. The dolls always smelled of that penetrating and horrible ceremony, perhaps, because of that, she hated perfumes, and they looked at her with their round blue pop eyes, at times lit up from the red, green, and yellow lights. She would get up and try to let down the blind; but the heat would suffocate her and she would end up stretched out on the bed, face down, until the sun cruelly woke her once again. Every night the music, the same music, the music from the hotel would reach her, from down there; the laughs of the customers who had drunk too much, or the quarrels, and always, always, always a music too syncopated, incomplete, cut up into fragments, the music of the Casa de los Negros. Each time that the doorman—she used to look down there, almost doubled over the window sill—would open the door and draw aside the bamboo curtain, the music would climb up the roof, as far as her window; she would be half out of her window, her braids falling heavily, "One day I'll cut my braids." Every week, once or twice, at night, Elena would let her come downstairs. Dionisia would dye her hair while she played solitaire.

"Learn to dye the roots of my hair, Marta. Dionisia has other things to be busy with. It's better for you to learn how," Dionisia explained harshly, her cigarette in her mouth.

"Look how it's done, wise up."

Elena would remain seated in her wrinkled chiffon nightgown, smelling overpoweringly of faded, numbing perfume. Dionisia would seize her long hair in her hands, dividing it into bundles. There was a savage and mean joy in all that as if some vengeance was directing her hands. She moved Elena's head nimbly, Elena, who, now and then moaned. She divided the hair into bunches and then, with a brush, she smeared it with a substance that turned white and foamy; the hair was no longer blond, but a muddy brown color mixed with grey. And Dionisia would say, "Do you see? Pay attention, Marta. You have to cover the roots, like this..."

She would observe. It's life—she thought—life which passes and doesn't return. And these two rats want to cut off my life, but I'll not tolerate it. She would look at her childish attire, her inappropriate braids, the curve Elena and Dionisia wanted to suppress, constrict, constrain, with garments that had something of medieval torture about them. "Don't be indecent, don't emphasize," Elena used to say in an exasperated tone. She had always been ready to slap her, especially lately. Her big hand with hard bones, always ready to fall on her cheek. While she would dye her hair, she thought, "There she is, with her slaps on the cheek; a wake of blows follows her the way foam follows ships. But one day I'll cut off my braids and in some way I'll humiliate her." For the slightest reason whatsoever she felt the sharp blow, the smack, the wounding laugh of Dionisia.

"Do you see, idiot? You've already ruined it."

Her wrath increased, an intolerable and excessive rancor, fermenting hatred, like yeast, in the seclusion of the room.

"Go read and practice your English," Elena would say yawning, next to the greenish glass eyes of the dolls dressed as Mme. Dubarry, Mme. Pompadour, Marie Antoinette, Louis XV, Cinderella, Marguerite Gautier—she named them this way—and, above all else, the one she loved best, the Hussar of the Guards, what an imbecilic and odd Hussar, with his corkscrew curls; and the others, monstrous parodies of chubby-cheeked girls, with their hard, swollen, plump cheeks painted red, perfumed, with the musty languor of falling chiffons. Whenever she was alone she would drag them over the floor. She would have attacks of stifled, solitary anger. Especially if Elena had slapped her.)

"I wasn't a girl," she repeated, with a distant pain. "But they wanted to prolong my childhood. I hampered them, both of them. They would have wanted to keep me on the shelf, like one of their horrible dolls."

"They?"

"Yes, my mother and Dionisia. Dionisia was her partner, friend, housekeeper; she was half in love with my father. And it was me she hated. She was my mother's right arm, her help. I realized that when Dionisia wasn't around, my mother was lost. She furnished the drugs, through her my mother met Raul. In the past (in her day) she had been a ship's stewardess and did the Shanghai-to-Marseilles run. She dealt in everything. Drugs, contraband... there was that little hotel and everything else, a cover-up. Roulette and poker included, were only the cover-up for the other thing."

She took another swallow and handed him her glass for him to fill it again. Suddenly he saw her, in some fantastic way, relieved of something.

"Talk to me. It will do you good."

She rubbed her ear slowly with her finger. He realized then that it was a customary gesture with her, something that instantly made her become childish and perplexed.

"And Raul was an unscrupulous, unskilled doctor, a voracious and stupid little animal, whom she was continuously calling into line. Elena fell in love with him. Desperately. She was mad, completely mad. She was about fifty and he had not yet reached thirty when I met him. The three of them followed the same course. They needed him and he knew how to pick a quarrel. My mother adored him. Raul did everything they wanted him to do, including drawing up death certificates for natural causes—when someone important wanted one. The three together seemed powerful. Raul provided young girls, almost children, to the old men customers at the hotel."

"Where was it?"

"In San Juan, near the border. But they had another hotel, a smaller one, in Irun. Raul was in charge there. Almost every day he would come by in his car. I got to know everything, little by little, by dint of hearing and listening, through wandering about like a soul in torment in the upper part of the hotel, by dint of putting my ear at the locks or by pretending to be asleep. I got acquainted with everything, filling myself up with everything, drop by drop, like a poison."

(In the darkness of the night the doors would creak. Dionisia had two beautiful and exasperating white cats. She learned to get around without her shoes, on tiptoe, in a rapid and slippery fashion. A narrow spiral staircase joined her attic-like room with the third floor landing. Her mother lived on the ground floor. She hated the cats and, often, when she would leave her room although forbidden to do so, she would stumble on of the cats—they were called Minou and Laka— and she would feel their soft and gentle rubbing, full of electricity, on her bare legs and hold back a cry of loathing. She would listen, hear, learn. The doors that she intentionally would leave partly closed upon leaving the room, the cracks of light, the dust filtering through, with the words, in a tiny and malignant dance in front of her eyes. Crouched down, at the hour when the two would get together with him in Elena's private sitting room, pressed against a dark corner, next to the peeling wall that she would slowly scrape with her finger, she would listen; and, at times, she would understand, and at times she would make up other stories that later would disturb her sleep. Then the deliberate sentences, the bantering half-words of the waiters and the maids. She was able to bathe in the ocean only very early in the morning when the hotel employees would go to the beach. She would see them stretch out in the sun, throw water on one another, shaking and laughing. She would remain, looking at them, detached and sad. One of them, a waiter called Rene, came close to her, furtively, two or three times. He would hold his hand out to her and invite her to go in the water with him. But she would run away, escape, and, suddenly, discover that she was afraid of people. Afraid of speaking, of answering questions. Rene's greenish eyes, his eyebrows covered with sparkling drops of water. A sensation of infinite dismay came over her, "I'm eighteen," she said to herself, full of amazement in front of the mirror, contemplating her delicate countenance, slightly tanned by the sea air, the blond braids, her big, pensive eyes. Her body, too, was attractive, her waist, her legs, her arms. The sun entered, marked an angle above her sides, obscurely, and the whitest area of her bathing suit became noticeable on her skin.

"Why can't I be like everybody else in the world, go where everybody else goes?" she shouted at her mother that night as she began to dye the roots of that harsh hair.

"Be quiet, you're a silly child."

Dionisia turned around to look at her. She held a burning black cigar in her lips and was piling up bills, sticking them on a nail, as sharp and hurtful as her glance.

"I'm not a girl, I'm already eighteen. No girl my age has to hide herself the way I do."

Dionisia let out a snicker through her cigar and Elena, turning her head covered with half-dyed curls, looked at her ill-naturedly and said:

"Well, Marta, I'm getting tired. Obey me."

And she added, more gently, "One day you'll thank me. Perhaps you might even be able to understand that: I only want to keep you from harm. Look, believe me, sweetie, understand that your mother wants you clean and pure as a dove. Life is hard, each one defends himself as he can, and it's for your own good. Mind me and don't bother me."

It was certain that she already knew a great deal. She would leave the door half-opened; she would huddle up and listen. At times a strange customer would arrive. They would open the high-ceilinged room for her, in the right wing, a twin of her own. She would remain a very short while, Raul would arrive, she would hear a muffled moaning which was very like Laka's mewing. On the following day, or hours later, the woman customer would leave, pale, her lips white. They would shut themselves up in the little sitting room; the woman would leave and they would never see her again. One day, an older man came with a girl, almost a child. The girl was complaining about something while they were going up the narrow spiral staircase. He slapped her. He said to Dionisia when she came to go through the girl's suitcase, "You're going to give this one a shot, aren't you?"

Instead of getting mad, Dionisia threw back her head and began to laugh.

"Be careful," she said to him. "You already know what can happen to you. But after all, it's a little operation and so far nothing has happened. Short of death everything has a remedy in this world."

That evening, when she was already lying down in bed, with the window open and the music coming up from the Casa de los Negros, the door of her room opened and Dionisia entered. She lit the lamp on the bedside table, a green, round eye, very close to her face. Dionisia sat down next to her and began to hug her legs.

"It's true, you're not a little girl, you're tight. They ought not to do this to you, Martita, poor little thing."

She didn't dare move. Dionisia kept hugging her legs, "You're sweet, Marta, if you could get dresses and be like the others."

Dionisia came and loosened the girl's braids. She took her to the mirror and combed her hair, long and blond, which fell down over her shoulders. Hair smooth and almost metallic in its brilliance. Dionisia said, "Look, little one, if you promise to be careful and mind me, I'll let you go out a little."

Her heart beat furiously, she didn't know whether from anger of from a wild joy.

"Yes, I promise, I want to live, Dionisia, I want to live."

Dionisia began to laugh and brought her face close to hers. In spite of her kindness there as no possibility of tenderness in her gestures, everything about her was angular, her bones stuck out noticeably, piercing, pushing out the flesh. She smelled of something unusual, almost medicinal, and said, "But be good and respectful to your poor mother. You know, child, when I met her she had already been through a lot. Do you remember the shop in Madrid?"

"Yes, I remember."

"Well, she built it up through her own effort; she had come out of nothing, the poor thing. But she has one weakness: men. She had, she still has, the ruination that comes from falling in love. When I met her, she was carrying you in her womb. And your father, a blond Milanese, handsome like you, had abandoned her. He was a real bastard, taking almost everything of hers with him, half-ruining her."

Dionisia remained pensive, her right hand in the air, holding the comb. She fixed her own hair and added.

"So we began, together. I had some money saved up and I was

tired. As you know I was then doing the Shanghai-to-Marseilles run; I had lived in Saigon for a time and in Macao, I had a lot of experience, some money and many friendships. I said to her, "Don't be stupid, Elena, pay attention to me." And we kept on with the shop, because it was a good cover-up for our real business."

"Which was?" she asked, pretending innocence. But Dionisia showed her yellow teeth, "You know very well, little thief."

"Will you let me try it?"

"Never, never for you. You still have to grow up a lot. And only if you promise me not to get spoiled by men."

"Why do you hate them?"

"Because they are filthy and crude."

"And Raul?"

"The worst of them. Your mother will pay very dearly for loving that dog. But he is clever, useful. He doesn't have a conscience and she adores him. Now go to sleep, child. Jump in bed and rest."

"And then? Tell me everything now that you have begun."

"Then we left the shop and set up the hotels. I have good contacts here in San Juan and Irun. I was the one who introduced her to Raul. At times I don't know whether to be happy about it or sorry. Raul is the difficult piece in this game, the one who might win the battle or lose it."

This last comment remained a little confusing. But it awoke in her a greater desire to know Raul. She saw him only from a distance, from the window, his light green Panford convertible in front of the Casa de los Negros; and, at times, his voice through the partition.

When Dionisia had left, her presence still remained there. And there was a great deal of mockery in the chubby-cheeked faces of Madame Pompadour, of the hideous Hussar, with his corkscrew curls and the mole on his cheek, all of them full of greasy rouge that Elena applied when she had a spell of feeling well. She got up, spit in their paces, one by one, until it seemed to her that she had no saliva left and that her palate and her tongue had dried up.

On another night Dionisia returned, with her stories and her hugs; and, once, brought with her a pretty dress, a woman's outfit.

"Where did you get it?"

"I'll take you with me tomorrow."

Suddenly a muffled rage filled her and she said, "I don't want to go anywhere with you; it's not like that, it's another prison."

Dionsia went into a rage and shouted, "Do as you're told, or it will be worse."

She didn't allow herself to be petted or have her hair combed, or be made up, as on other occasions. Dionisia said, "You'll soon calm down."

She slapped her, took away the dress, the rouge, the perfume. Minou and Laka were pushing against the door. They wanted in. She heard their claws scratching against the wood of the door. They were complaining like that girl on whom they had performed a simple operation.)

Sanamo entered and took away the darkness. She and Manuel looked at each other like strangers. Something between them appeared to have broken.

7

"Getting acquainted with everything, drop by drop, like a poison," Manuel repeated, trying to get her talking again. "I also know about that."

Marta nodded weakly. The wine, light and pink, began to sink into her with a soft heaviness which perhaps could be beneficial.

(The spiral staircase, dark and twisting, in the corner where Laka's eyes shone like phosphorescent buttons...barefoot and wrapped in her bathrobe, she went down to the third floor landing with its pots of dwarf palm trees. She crossed the door of the private room, the dark corridor, and there it was, the little back door of her mother's sitting room. The glass transom which lately she had come to know so well. It was a door they never opened. It was very dark and she used a stepladder to creep up to the transom. She raised the burnished glass, put the little stick on the transom frame, looked through the open crack and saw them, heard them. Him especially, with more attention and curiosity. Above his shoulders and above the back of his neck, which was covered with curly and shiny hair, there was something powerful and surprising about him. And she remembered, *they're rough and brutal*. At times they argued. She made out only outlines of people and furniture. They seemed to flutter from time-to-time, a motion that made her half-close her eyes. At other times distant voices reached her, as though lost in a distant country. The springs shook, and once, Raul's feet came close to her field of vision, bare, dark, almost black, like the carpet. They were the feet of a mysterious and unknown animal. *I have never seen a man close up*. When Dionisia entered the sitting room they reviewed their accounts, drank, argued. The smoke from their cigarettes rose to the edge of the transom where she was getting drowsy. She kept her body stuck to the wall, even though it seemed full of needles. But her curiosity and desperation were stronger than her fatigue. She remained there, a sentinel, and could hear how Dionisia was saying to Raul, "You're putting on a big belly, getting bald, my friend. When I met you, you looked like a Greek god and now, what? a pompous gentleman, sweaty and big-bellied." These jokes didn't please Raul and he answered either with gross remarks or with an Olympian disdain. In any case it seemed, in some way, that he was afraid of Dionisia. "He was a pretty guy, Dionisia would say, "What they call a mama's boy. And what's more, dreaming of medicine in the service of humanity, no? Didn't you say that?" She spoke like this when there was something between them having to do with business, with money, that got them both excited. Especially Raul. That day he threw a chair and she began to hear his footsteps stifled in the carpet, like blows, and Elena's distant entreaties: "Don't get carried away, don't upset each other, God, I beg of you, let's have a little peace." And then she heard the hard and wounding laughter of Dionisia.

At that moment something gave way. The odious Laka delicately slipped between her legs, shoving her. She lost her balance and tried to grasp the clamps of the transom, but she couldn't. She was like a dream wrapped up in smoke. She fell and a great noise left the argument in suspense on the other side of the door. She remained on the floor, filled with fear. Without knowing why she imagined Raul's dark feet against the floor, she heard footsteps and the little table that was in front of the door being pushed aside. Then all the light, heavy and square, fell upon her as if the light of the room had been changed into a yellowish block broken off from the recently discovered door frame. She closed her eyes and felt herself being carried and moved by an arm. She heard a harsh and stifled voice, like the footsteps on the carpet of that room, the muzzled cry of a voice that came out from clamped teeth. They dragged her to the center of the room while she obstinately kept her eyes closed. She heard Dionisia's sudden and harsh laugh and Raul's voice asking, "Who's she? A maid?" as he continued shaking her.

But her mother snatched her from his arms. Immediately she felt herself pulled close against her mother's flaccid breast that was covered with wrinkled muslin; the gold cross her mother always wore dug into her cheek. Her mother's hands pressed down on her as though to perforate her arms. She heard the trembling of her mother's voice, "Let her alone, Raul. She's a child, a little girl."

"But who is she?"

"It's her daughter," vociferated Dionisia.

At that moment she dared open her eyes and saw Dionisia's yellow teeth laughing maliciously and savagely, screeching like metal on a piece of marble. Elena was pale, and all her wrinkles suddenly stood out in the furrows of her mouth made up falsely in the form of a heart, her eyes enormous and heavy with mascara and eyeliner, her dilated irises like black stars wandering strangely like extinguished stars.

"She's a child," she repeated two more times. She pressed the child against herself. But it was not love, it was a bestial desire to hide her, to undo her, perhaps to return her to the womb where she should never have breathed. She said to herself at that moment—and it astonished her to have that thought, exactly at that moment—*why, then why wasn't a simple operation performed?* At the same time there was a terrible, obscure cry that arose, like water from the earth, like imprisoned and violent water, a cry that said, "I want to live, I want to live."

She freed herself from that arm, which was in the way of love, and said, "I am not a child and I hate you." She spit on the floor and a terrible wrath filled her. She turned toward Raul and saw him for the first time. It was something surprising, strange and unknown, almost fearful, in front of her. Life was looking at her. He was much taller than he appeared to be from the window—*I always saw him from a bird's-eye view*—and a desire to laugh almost took hold of her because he was looking at her with an immense amazement, a wisp of hair falling down over his forehead and those dark eyes, such as she had never seen, so full of blackness that the cornea could hardly be seen; and the tanned skin, the shirt undone over a powerful neck which had already surprised her while prying at the transom and then, a hidden flash of lightning shook her from top to bottom. She began to laugh.

"What are you laughing about, stupid?" asked Dionisia. But she, too, was laughing and Raul imitated her. That mouth of fleshy lips and the enormous teeth. She remembered a story that she had read as a child where there was a cannibal who had that same mouth and she thought, *He's a cannibal, with white fangs like a dog.* His heavy, dark laughter dragged across the floor, like his unshod feet. On his wrist he wore a chain with something hanging on it that had an engraved number. Raul raised his hand to his forehead and let himself fall into the armchair, laughing. The only one who was not laughing was her mother, who suddenly advanced toward her with her muslin floating in some invisible wind, the wind of her own steps impelled by wrath, fear, desperation of her faded dreams, impelling her. She came close to her and slapped her once, twice, then three times, until Raul grabbed her, pulled her aside, and in turn pressed her against him as he said, "Why Elena, why?" Why is it so important? It's a girl's prank."

And suddenly, in that body half close to her own there also occurred the same suppressed, muzzled flash of lightning. It lasted only for a second, yet there fell a contained silence which was burning and brutal. Thus, suddenly, their two bodies met, one against the other; and all her being molded and adapted itself to that other warm form. It was something new and distinct that the human body never understood until that moment. With amazement, she contemplated her own arms around Raul's waist and her densely compressed breast against his back, protecting her from Elena. And Elena was there, only a pale and perfumed scarecrow lashed by an inefficient wind, with her shining tears that were not damp, and her mouth open in a voiceless scream, while Raul said, "Let her be. Everything's all right. Don't touch her."

Then Dionisia, with great gentleness, took her from him. It was painful to be separated from that body, from that warm contact.

Dionisia said, "But you're going around half-naked."

Her hand pressed inside his hand which also resisted letting go. And while Dionisia, with an insincere kindness, separated it from the body there was almost a call, a persistent voice. It seemed to her that they tore off a trunk to which they belonged. Raul's hand, big, dark and soft, held her; the more their bodies were separated the more their hands remained bound together. And, upon being separated, they remained connected, their two arms stretched out one to the other like a bridge, gripping each other's hands, as they followed the call and the voice forming irreductibly, in spite of the other sweetness, and of the tears and confusion of the poor perfumed ghost who suddenly seemed like the poor Hussar of the Guards with his faded curls. And she thought, *the poor Hussar has grown old.*

With the back of her hand Elena struck a blow (like the one she once saw a cook give a rabbit on the back of the neck in order to kill it) on their two linked hands and split with one stroke that bridge which was a sentence without words stretched between her and Raul. The two old women floated excitedly like two shadows around the two of them, unexpectedly young, suddenly young, awakening between walls papered with violets and hyacinths.

Raul said, "yes, it's all right now. I don't know how you can do that to a poor child. Let her quiet down, go and sit down, dear."

Elena threw herself headfirst onto the sofa and began to weep. Dionisia rushed over to stroke her neck. She saw ancient and enormous deception in Dionisia's eyes. But it was a far-off and gentle deception, like the smile of ancient statues lost in abandoned foliage. Dionisia said, "Well, Elena, does it matter?"

Raul sat down, remote and even ugly, and lit a cigar. Suddenly she felt like saying, *I hate all three of you, you seem horrible and malignant, like octopi. You're ugly, I despise you and you are old.*

But Dionisia said, "It's because she doesn't want this poor girl to be involved with the people who swarm around here."

Raul answered, "It's not necessary for her to get involved, but there's no reason for her to be hidden as though she were the devil's monster." And, upon saying this, he turned toward her. And in his eyes there was something black and on fire which, at other times, had repelled her.

She forgot the softness of his skin, his body against hers, and said, "Let me go."

"Go," moaned Elena, "and don't come downstairs until I call you. Don't come downstairs because I don't want to see you for several days."

She waited in vain for Raul's or Dionisia's protest. But Dionisia kept on stroking Elena's neck, with odiously sweet hands. And Raul, with his veiled eyelids, continued smoking his cigar. The light shone and changed color on the chain hanging from his wrist, the strange number engraved inside the medallion attached to it.

She went up to her room, slowly, as though dreaming; and as soon as she got to the spiral staircase, began to weep. She noticed tears falling on her cheeks and was aware of an enormous humiliation that couldn't be defined. It was not humiliation for having been slapped in front of a stranger or for having been surprised in something shameful, like spying on lovers, hearing the conversations of others, or for having been treated like a child. It was more a profound humiliation that she didn't know how to describe and which burned her like a scalding iron. She was in the dark contemplating the flashing red and green of the cigarette sign of the Casa de los Negros on the chubby cheeks of the Hussar of the Guards. She sat in a corner of the room, one moment green, one moment red, one moment black, until she went to bed.

On the following day Dionisia sent her a message with a maid. "They say you should come downstairs, Miss, to have a cup of coffee with everyone in the garden."

And there they were, the three of them, waiting for her; Raul, her mother and Dionisia. After that, they called her every day, and she began an hour of intimacy with them. She did not know whether taking part in it satisfied her or not.

The summer was reaching its end. Once again September was approaching. In the garden the iron chairs, wet from rain, were dripping under the last rays of the sun. There she was, her mother, and he, Raul, (rarely worn out and sad) with his renewed interest for newspapers, for news and politics. Elena was complaining about something.

"I don't know what's wrong with me...," she said.

She observed them silently as though spying, like an animal. On the lawn two birds were chasing one another. Raul was looking at her and not at her mother.

"How old are you now?"

She smiled. She looked at herself in the mirror, coldly, briefly. She knew that she was pretty. Her mother gave them a peevish glance.

"She's a child...Do you hear what I'm saying, Raul? At this time every year I get this way..."

She wants him to ask her something, to listen to her stupid remarks. But, instead of doing so, he began looking obstinately at the lawn of well-tended and damp grass. A bellhop in a red uniform came up with the evening papers under his arm.

"Moreover," Elena continued insistently, "I always know beforehand what's going to happen to me. I foresee it and I can't avoid it."

She turned her head and looked at her. "She's withered and looks like her nose has grown bigger from smelling stupid things."

"That happens to all of us," said Raul, not even bitterly. He spoke like that just to speak, just to follow tiredly her train of thought. Something was on his mind and it kept him far from there; and she realized it.

Elena looked at him, with a nervous eyelid.

"We're old," she said. "Horrible old people of forty or thirty...Not like those little old people who walk around here, giving crumbs to the sparrows. No, we're horrible old people of thirty or forty."

Not true, she thought, even though she was not deprived of her recently abandoned childish logic, *she's forty-nine, he's twenty-eight.* She looked more attentively at her mother, taking a sip from her cup. Indeed, the worse thing was that her mother was sad. He remained quiet, his hands crossed over his stomach. In his lips a cigar burned and covered his face with its smoke.

"And, that's the way we like to be."

Raul violently rubbed one eye. *He's afraid of conjunctivitis*, she thought. *Mama has just had it and perhaps he fears catching it. It's certain that they are old and miserable, old rats of thirty or forty.* She looked at her mother more attentively. She was half-reclined in her chaise longue, her hair dyed, parted in two, falling like golden and persistent water on each side of her face. Her eyelids were wide and well-outlined, amber in tone, and her eyes were of an ill-defined color. At that moment she was neither ugly nor pretty. She was her mother. But for some time she knew she didn't love her, that she had never loved her, that she had nothing to do there, in front of her in her rocking chair, with her long hands always in the foreground to make their beauty evident. *I would like to hate her*, she thought apathetically. *She says things that are weak, and stupid. Things that she reads, or even worse, that she supposes can be read somewhere. There's always someone who's written or is going to write what she says. And, to top it off, she's not pleasant unless she's had a glass too many of what prolongs her euphoria. With her, everything turns out useless, not even stupid. I would like to hate her, give her a kick you know where and say to her, "go away from here." But she's my mother and something I don't even understand holds me back.*

Raul smiled and said, "Dear."

She got up and kissed them, rapidly, on the cheek. First her, then him. He held her for a moment by the arm, gently. She felt close to his smell, his harsh, black shining hair.

"Where are you going?"

"Over there."

"Go to bed early," said Elena. "Don't wander off somewhere. You've very thin."

Almost no one remained in the hotel. From that part of the hotel you could see the public square. Tradesmen's families, workers, office workers, advanced slowly toward the sea. That's true, it's a holiday, she remembered. It's some saint's day. White and flaccid flesh inadequately dressed; pale flesh with marks of undershirts, of ample and cheap bras, advanced slowly toward the sea. Swallows were flying low, with strange cries, spreading a mysterious joy over life.

The entrance to the Casa de los Negros was there, in front of and below her window, in the side alley of the hotel. The facade was painted a rabid white and the double row of dwarf palms stood at the door. From above the floors and the windows the terraces, the cables crossing back and forth, and the illuminated letters from all corners of the night seemed to be born. She leaned halfway out her window to look down far enough to contemplate the Casa de los Negros. She often saw the blacks of the orchestra in their red and gold jackets with musical instruments in their cases, like mysterious and mute animals, going in and coming out. *Something's going on somewhere; something I don't know what it is, something that shrieks at me, too.* The humid September heat stuck to her skin, soaked everything like a persistent vapor. Inside the almost opaque globes of iridescent glass the light vibrated, like the sky during a storm. I'll go downstairs and I'll leave at night. The immense, luminous globes, like pearls, like giant eyes, invited her. She thought she heard the echo of a long and metallic lament. *I like the trumpets.* She distinguished the palm trees down below, black, almost blue. Not the slightest breeze was blowing, everything was quiet and penetrated by the echo of that music which, more then being heard, was guessed at. She looked for her sandals. She looked at herself in the mirror, she hated her ridiculous clothes, her braid wound around her head. She looked for her scissors and suddenly cut it. Her hair fell, flaccid, uneven, around her neck. Under her blond, almost silvery bangs, her eyes appeared enormous, almost surprised. *The Milanese was very blond, the Milanese pig that made me.* She ran her finger over the rim of her mouth, suddenly she remembered the rouge that Dionisia had brought her. She looked for it and put it on her mouth. Her eyes and eyebrows shone more forcefully. She brushed her hair that fell awkwardly, poorly cut. In her face was something stupid and savage. There, in the mirror, half her face was on fire, suddenly red, then suddenly green. Her sandals fit her feet awkwardly, her hands trembled. "The reason is that she doesn't want you to be corrupted," Dionisia had once said. *But what's sure is that she doesn't want them to see this girl so grown-up, so pretty.* The sky appeared reddish, somewhat orangeish above the blackness of the roofs. The palm trees seemed like an immobile procession of venerable beings, guardians of something, haughty for some reason. *I'm going, I'm fed up with all this, I'm leaving and going to take a walk around here someplace.* Somewhere, above the expected sound of the sea, a scream broke out, calling to her.

She went downstairs by the spiral staircase, crossed through the two apartments with an air of feigned indifference. She imagined glances, dark and tiny tunnels, crossing the air toward her. In the little sitting room someone was playing poker. *Dionisia taught me to play poker. Lately Mama doesn't control the trembling of her lips. Her dry mouth horrifies me, her mouth under the color of the rouge, you can count the wrinkles around her eyes. And, yet, she is beautiful, she pretends that her mouth is smaller, almost heart-shaped. She looks ugly to me. I prefer her mouth un-made-up, the way she had it on the beach. When she's at the beach she appears to be a different woman. When she stays on the beach, forgotten, perhaps without thinking of anything, with her eyes closed, under the sun. It's not that at that moment that she seems younger, but in her stretched out, tired body, there's a sweetness that abandons her as soon as she gets up, gets dressed, gets made-up. At times pleasure makes her look old.* Lately she had been drinking quite a bit. At times Raul was more than a week late in coming. "I wasn't able to come, I assure you," he'd say. She hated them. She knew about their arguments, their odious intimacy that disturbed her. *I don't want to be that way. I'll never be old.* She left the house, crossed the sidewalk. Among the palm trees the night was getting darker. On the other side rose up the Casa de los Negros. *Perhaps they won't let me in.*

Then she saw him next to the light-green Panhard. All her rebellion rose up in the heat of her cheeks. She drew near, her mind made up. He looked at her, just looked at her, he didn't even move. She crossed the street and drew nearer. He looked like a puppet.

"Yes, it's me." she said.

She was drowning in some kind of hate that she couldn't even identify. It was a feeling so distant and old, like the noise she thought she heard, at times drawing near and at others going away, during the long, heavy, lingering night up there in the dormer window of the hotel. Raul looked at her seriously and almost pleasantly. She walked up to him and said, "Yes, it's me, you're not dreaming, it's me and don't say anything to her."

Unexpectedly Raul began to laugh.

"One night I ran away. I was fed up with my mother treating me like a little girl, hiding me like an affront. I felt like getting out of that inhuman confinement. I met him, Raul, and he said to me, "That's natural, poor little thing, come up with me. Don't be afraid." That's how everything began."

The interior curtain of the Casa de los Negros was made of bamboo. She almost jumped, surprising herself, and finally, she parted the bamboo curtain. She heard a little noise above her head, around her shoulders, like a very slight colliding of bones. A pleasant fear shook her. With her two arms she separated the long bamboo fringes and went in. Raul followed very closely. Without seeing him she noticed his smile of an accomplice with closed lips, floating about the edges of his mouth. He looked for her hand, seized it, and led her through the sonorous darkness where, amid a golden smoke, little pink and green lights were moving about.

Raul said, "Come this way, let's have a drink."

Something got tangled between her feet. But it was something without a body, rather like a gust of wind that drags along the crackling leaves. Raul said something in her ear, so that his very low voice should reach her through the sharp metallic sound of the trumpet.

"Tell me what you want to drink."

Although she noticed that his eyes were asking about something else.

"Anything's fine, I'm not acquainted with anything."

"That's not true," he said. His shoulder pressed gently against her. They were next to a little, white, round table where a little pink flame was burning. Her eyes were suddenly filled with tears, everything came to her as if through a polished crystal.

"Why are you crying? Don't be afraid."

8

There were two rows of flower pots on both sides of the door of the Casa de los Negros.

"Where are you going?" asked Raul.

"Inside there."

"Then it's better for you to go with me."

He grasped her by the arm. She looked up close at his profile. He had a short nose with large nostrils. Something savagely animal cried out in his whole person, filled it with a troubled and pleasant feeling. He dragged her from her narrow isolation. *I am totally unacquainted with those beings, with those Dionisia foretells about and less brutality and an evil smelling mouth.*

Without preambles, as if he were waiting for the first chance to ask, he said, "What is there between you and Dionisia?"

She looked at him in silence. Then, rapidly, he changed the topic.

"Who cut your hair? What do I see? Something unusual is going on with you."

"I cut it. I know now that it's a bad job, but that doesn't matter to me."

Raul passed his hand over her head, smoothing the hair on the two sides of her face, arranging it behind her ears.

"We'll see what your mother says tomorrow."

"It doesn't matter to me what she might say."

She didn't want him to notice the unusual fantasy that was born from the touch of that hand.

"I'm not the least bit afraid," she said. "I'm crying because at long last I'm going to the Casa de los Negros."

"This is not called the Casa de los Negros. But I like the name. Well, you can see that there is nothing peculiar about it."

"No, but I've gone in, I'm here, and from now on I'll go wherever I want."

She asked for something and the waiters brought some drinks.

Raul said, "You're going to tell me the whole business about Dionisia now."

"I don't feel like it."

An unusual fear returned. Afraid that he would leave, that everything would be over. She looked around her, *It's true, it doesn't have anything peculiar about it.* She probably said so without seeing what it was, and now she realized it. A small room, a long, white piano, and the platform with the blacks where the instruments that they had taken out of their cases shone. A heavy silence prevailed; only the piano was heard. A fat black man was picking out a broken melody and drops of sweat were shining on his forehead. Under the pink spotlight the waiter's long and hairy hand seized the bottle and poured the liquid into the glasses. On the table was a small piece of cardboard with the number 23. He took hold of it and began to turn it around in his fingers.

"She says that you're a good girl," Raul pointed out.

"I am. I am good."

Raul kept smiling without scarcely moving his cannibal-like thick and prominent lips.

"I am going to explain something to you," she suddenly said. Like a torrent her own voice intoxicated and excited her. "Dionisia promised to help on the condition that I wouldn't get spoiled by any man."

Raul gave out a small and hissing laugh.

"Dionisia told me you help her smoke."

"Yes. She taught me to fill her pipe. It's more convenient that way. If she has to do it herself, the effect between pipes is weakened."

"Do you do it well?"

They both appeared very amused. It reminded her of her early childhood at the beach with a boy. Stretched out, one on each side of the sand castles where they were digging a tunnel, their hands sought each other out; and, with their hands intertwined, they began to tell one another mysterious things about grown-ups, which made them laugh until they cried. Thus it was with Raul at that moment.

"At times she comes upstairs and says, be still, girl, don't cry out. Prepare a pipe for me. She opens her little lacquer box, lights the little crystal lamp, with its cute little flame. It's fun. I take the vial with its syrup and make a little ball, very small, at the end of the rod. Then I put it in the little container…. She says it's made of the best quality brass and that a mandarin gave it to her as a present. She has these obsessions. She says that not all the brass types give the same aroma, that hers is the best container there is. Fine. It's amusing to hear what she says. She's very refined. She stretches out, her eyes swollen. It seems very funny to me to see her. I asked her once, "What are you feeling?" And she said to me, "I'm directing my dreams, girl. Then she turns the container around, draws it near the flame and begins to suck.... Almost immediately I have to clean it with a black pin and twirl it to refill it. About three times. Thanks, love, she says to me. When she lived there she had a servant for that. Now she has me."

She let loose a little burst of laughter and looked at him.

"It seems all right to me," said Raul. His fixed and glassy eyes shone next to the lampshade. The pupils of his eyes had become smaller and turned an amber color. She thought, *didn't he have black eyes?*

"Did she let you try it?"

"No. Not yet."

The sound of the piano stopped. A great silence descended, wandering back and forth, fragmented and floating in the noise of the conversations.

But suddenly the trumpet crossed from one side to the other of the Casa de los Negros.

Raul said, "Let's dance."

"I don't know how to dance."

"That makes no difference. Just follow. I'll lead."

She followed him again and pressed against his body thinking about now and remembering the first time in her mother's sitting room. Consciously she squeezed against him and discovered that she had waited for a long time for that search and for that meeting. Raul's hand stroked her shoulder, softly.

"Let yourself be carried away."

The powerful slow music made the darkness vibrate. Perhaps a scream, like an immense spider of burnished metal, ran across the invisible walls of the Casa de los Negros. She was clumsy, her feet tripped and got tangled in Raul's. They were laughing again, she didn't know why. He said something she didn't understand. But she laughed. It was easy.

"How old are you really?" Raul said through the great din, leading her once more to the table.

"Eighteen."

"I once saw a photo of you," he said, lighting a cigarette. "You were about ten, very pretty, with your short braids."

He stretched out his hand again and stroked her hair once more. Then his hand softly grazed her ear. She remained rigid, holding back her breath. She thought: *I have heard love spoken about. I don't know whether this is it.* But she didn't believe that love could be a thing like this, dense, nailed down like an old root, without any tenderness. *After all is said and done it doesn't matter much to me, love is probably something dark and thick, like syrup.* The thought made her laugh and smile.

"Do you know what I remember now? What my mother said to me this evening, when she said good-bye to me. She said, "Go to bed early."

Her own laugh was something tangible and alive, there before her own eyes, above the white tablecloth. Raul's hand caressed her neck. *If I let that hand escape I have lost the world. I have to hold on to it.* Raul brought his face close to hers and kissed her gently on the cheek. His skin was delicate and smooth, almost like that of a girl's, near the temple where his hair began.

"Dear papa," she said, repeating her own laugh. Raul covered her mouth and his laugh seemed to be hers, drowned in hers. Once again he reminded her of the little boy on the beach, their hands intertwined through the tunnel in the sand.

"Let's get away from here," Raul said.

"I don't want to leave yet."

She wasn't afraid. What she didn't want was to end the night so soon. She imagined Raul's sudden impatience and said to herself, *I don't feel that the night should be spoiled for me, just like that. It has to last.*

"But everything here has already been seen," insisted Raul. "There's not much more to be seen."

"Then let's go to another place."

"Where, dear?" he said. "Let's go home. Let's go to your room."

"No. Let's go some place or another."

They had a couple of drinks more. Then, suddenly, Raul turned somber and not very talkative. She felt the weight of his clear and dense eyes, as though bathed in honey. The alcohol filled her with a pleasant excitement.

"You're pretty," Raul said. "Much more than can be seen at first sight. You have a hidden beauty that can only be seen at the end of a great deal of time, after seeing and speaking with you."

The music was noisy again.

"I would very much like to know how to dance. Really and truly I'd like to."

"Good," he said. "You can learn that immediately."

And, almost without transition, he added, "Let's go."

There was no choice but to follow him through the darkness, the bamboo, the doorman's smile.

"Good-bye, Snowball," said Raul. He put his arm around her shoulders as though it were cold out.

"What an ugly dress you're wearing. Truly it's not right. You could be the prettiest woman in the world."

He looked at her with a new attentiveness, almost with curiosity.

"Now your hair appears white," he said. "Under these lights it's like silver."

They walked to the Paso del Mar. It seemed that there was no ground under the soles of her feet. Raul's arm was like a steel ring around her neck and she thought, *this is what I want, exactly this, and she is going to be left without him because I'm going to take him from her. Perhaps love might not be this, but hatred is.*

They reached the sea. They went down to the beach and she immediately felt her sandals filling with sand. It was sticking to her soles, between her toes. She took off her sandals. And, the minute she did so Raul put his arms around her and she felt his sharp teeth on her mouth and neck.

"Good, let's go home," she said quietly.

They went like two thieves, on tiptoe, silently. She went upstairs first. And, upon starting up the spiral staircase and thinking of the new hatred that filled her, she again felt a brutal joy. The treads creaked, as if some mysterious little corpse were shut up inside the treads, complaining like diminutive coffins where stray cats meow or cats drown in the river. She silently laughed.

She entered slowly and softly opened the door. Only then did she realize that she had left her sandals on the beach and was walking around barefoot. She left the door ajar, without turning on the lights. She sat down on the bed. She still felt the soles of her feet covered with a thin layer of sand. The electric sign of the Casa do los Negros seemed an enormous wink of complicity. She rubbed her hands on the soles of her feet and heard the light rain of sand against the wood of the floor. Raul pushed open the door, entered, and closed it carefully behind him. She closed her eyes and stretched out, gently.

"That night Raul came up to my room and that was repeated during many nights; all of which lasted for the summer. My mother didn't suspect anything. At least she didn't suspect anything about me. And I suppose that Dionisia didn't either. I learned to pretend very well. Since that moment everything was a continuous pretense. But I confess that I had a lot of trouble keeping it up. The fact is, all my life I have been lying, sometimes voluntarily, sometimes involuntarily."

(Lately Elena had been saying frequently, "As soon as winter arrives, you'll be able to have a different life. I'll send you away, you'll see, you'll get acquainted with people. You'll get married, perhaps..."

A strange eagerness had gotten into her. She no longer hid it; rather, she wanted to get her away from her side. Raul frequently went to Irun where they had their other hotel.

One day he said naturally, "Elena, I'm going to take the little one with me to Irun so that she can enjoy herself a little."

"To Irun? With you? I don't know what distraction that can be for her."

"Let her go to the movies... or whatever. I go and come during the day, you know. Let her buy a dress or something, something a little nice."

Dionisia was playing solitaire at the next table. A cigar was burning in her mouth and she cast a glance at them, rapid and vague.

"Why not?" Dionisia said unexpectedly. "Why not, Elena? Look at the kind of clothes she has. She looks like a beggar."

Autumn was already at hand. The hotel remained empty. The day appeared grey and unpleasant.

Elena was pensive for a moment:

"All right, if she wants, let her go. But don't take her to the hotel. Leave her in some other place."

"Of course." Raul opened his newspaper like a paper screen which hid him almost entirely. "Can you believe that it hadn't occurred to me before? Let her go to the movies, shopping, or whatever she wants. And then I'll go by and pick her up. If she has to go away this winter she has to learn how to smarten up. And you don't want to go with her, as far as I can see."

"I can't." Elena's cigarette trembled in her lips. In her enormous eyes grew a strange emptiness.

She remained quiet, almost without breathing. Under the table she felt Raul's leg against hers. The newspaper crackled, making a strange noise that made Elena blink rapidly. Raul raised his head.

"And go to the beauty parlor," Dionisia said. "Since the last disaster you committed, you do look like a daub."

She ran her hand through her hair. She felt it silky and soft. And her heart against her breast, like a door knocker.

After dinner it began to rain with greater force. It wasn't the customary pitter-patter, it was almost a deluge.

"Don't go out in weather like this," Elena said through the steam from her coffee.

The three of them were once more in the sitting room. On the wall the wallpaper of violets and hyacinths looked like grimaces. The pearly light of the rain crossed the window panes, the window curtains of pink gauze. Something lucid and terrible was born in her, she discovered the trembling of Elena's lips, *the beginning of defeat, of triumph.* Dionisia's sadness, indecipherable, went from one to the other.

She said, "Yes, I'm going. But…," in Elena's voice an anguished weakness throbbed. "But, child, it's pouring down."

She didn't even answer her. She had scarcely finished her coffee before she went up to her room to get ready. When she came down she said, "Give me some money."

Elena was looking for something in the drawers of her desk. She looked at her beautiful white hands, enormous. Her lacquered nails, also enormous. She was tall, white and heavy. She spoke to her without looking at her, slowly. There was something hidden in her voice, and she could not define whether it was fear or a very wary suspicion, full of all the experience which she lacked.

She said, "I'm thinking that you'll go to work," she said. "I'm going to send you to Madrid this winter. You'll work, you'll learn what it is to earn one's livelihood, to fight…. You know, Marta, I mistakenly thought of making you into a little lady. It's useless. At first I wanted to give you an education. But you didn't turn out to be intelligent. You're lazy and stupid, but I swear you'll learn what work is.

"Very well. Are you going to give me the money or not?"

Her mother turned around quickly. The two of them were alone in the room and, suddenly, she looked at her as she would any other woman. She was no longer the submissive little Marta, with her blond braids, not more important or trembling than Laka. The eyes she saw in her when she looked at some determined woman.

"Yes, take it. Buy what you want, dress like a whore, if you like. I see that all I did to keep you from evil is useless. You know, Marta, in spite of everything, I pity you because you are still very innocent. Put on make up. Go to the beauty parlor. You don't have good taste. You are gross, selfish and rude like your father."

It was the first time that she had spoken of him and she thought, *the Milanese pig.*

She stretched out her hand, without knowing what to say. Her mother handed her a little white envelope. She was tempted to tear it open right there, but she restrained herself. *There's time.*

A thin ray of light began to play on the wall paper. She cried out, with a voice of triumph.

"You see? It's no longer raining."

She turned halfway around without saying good-bye, pushed the door—it remained open behind her, like a great yawn—and ran downstairs, clutching in her hand the little white envelope. The entire garden was shining, damp, under the metallic sun. She heard a dog bark and then the long whistle of the train and the odor of the damp earth was carried to her eager nose, like a shrieking wind. She looked toward Raul's window. A bird flew toward the eaves.

A little later Raul came downstairs, his hair damp, shiny, and too much smoothed down. His skin was still burned by the sun of the recently disappeared summer. It was turning an olive, almost dirty color. A lighter spot stood out on his nose. *He's ugly*, she thought.

"Your face is peeling," she said to him.

He rubbed his nose as he threw his briefcase on the back seat.

She slammed the car door, the way one does when they close something with definiteness. *A period, an age, a world, whatever it might be.* And then they pulled out and veered toward the Paseo del Mar and turned onto the highway between two rows of trees. *It's true,*

I didn't turn out to be very intelligent. I have never liked studying. And when I read I don't grasp what the book is saying. I get tired, I get bored. I like music, life, the trees, the sky. Something is alive there, waiting for me.

Upon making the turn around the hotel she saw Dionisia through the window grating. Dressed in black, her long face of a French-Basque woman, her arms falling down alongside her body. She seemed like a dignified scarecrow. She supposed that she would still be running around a lot before she gave up thinking about what she was leaving behind. But she had said good-bye to everything.)

"One afternoon we went to Irun on a pretext. We spent three days together, without seeing anybody."

(She didn't know sadness. Bored or desperate, full of joy or of impotent wrath, she had not known what sadness was until that morning, when the second day dawned. She woke up. The scream of the seagulls entered through the open window. They were in a small and sordid hotel near the fishing village of Fuente-arrabia. The room, in one of the lower floors of the dirty-grey, narrow building, was much larger than the room of the hotel in San Juan. The light entered in stripes through the cracks of worm-eaten and faded wood, through the Venetian blinds that were fastened together by a latch that couldn't be adjusted and that were pushed by the wind. The monotonous and annoying complaint of the old wood seemed to scream like the seagulls. For some reason that she didn't understand why Elena had said "Don't take her to the hotel." "Of course," he had answered. But there they were, in Raul's room, big and poorly furnished, with its old chairs of red plush, worn out and dirty at the headrest. She understood the real purpose of that hotel ruled by Raul as she understood that of the hotel in San Juan. *Let's go to the hotel. It doesn't make any difference, what else is there for us? Try not to make any noise. No one will be able to find us. Elena won't come. Why? How do you know? She won't come, I know that, she never comes, Dionisia perhaps, but Dionisia doesn't frighten me.* Her heavy and thick tongue refused to speak.

Barefooted, crossed over the carpet of dirty red velvet with big splotches of alcohol or of some other corrosive liquid. They were strange islands they tried not to step on, so that the soles of their bare feet might not be contaminated by something viscous and disgusting, even though she didn't know what. There was the desk of waxed and shiny wood, looking too new in the dust, and the light fixture of white and red glass. Raul remained stretched out, asleep, almost black against the sheet. Only the gold chain on his wrist shone palely. Lying on his side, his head buried in the pillow, his thick cheek, like a bulky package, his eyes tightly closed, frowning in two deep furrows between the eyebrows that almost grew together. She bent over him, Raul's arm fell to one side of the bed. She stooped over as far as she could to decipher the sign on the medal that hung from his neck. He was asleep, totally asleep; she heard the tenuous whistle of his half-opened mouth. She brought her face close to his. He smelled repugnantly of stale, acid, alcohol. She went to the desk. The little key was hanging, shining from the lock. The seagulls were shrieking and she thought *It will surely rain.* She was afraid he might wake up, so she turned the key softly. The roll top of the desk of joined with small rods rolled back like the broad tongue of a snake into its mouth. On the green cloth she found the photograph album and opened it. Girls smiled from their cardboard frames. Girls with makeup, scarcely thirteen, fourteen, fifteen years of age. Like the dolls in her room, the Hussar of the Guard, with their chubby cheeks. Some wore sailor costumes, a braid on their shoulders, curled bangs of dolls kept in a rancid closet. She slowly closed it and returned to the bed. The balcony cast more and more light on the room. She felt her mouth clammy, her eyes troubled, an unexpected desire to vomit. *I'll never be able to love anybody*—she thought, filled with uneasiness—*no one, not even myself, not even my childhood memories. Someone says that childhood is always remembered with love, but I already know nothing of that, only curiosity and desire. I have heard Dionisia and Raul speak about love. He tells me, "I love you." At times he says so. It's not true, but they say, perhaps it's a habit. Loving someone must be such a strange thing, as Dionisia says that my mother loved the Milanese. Perhaps that's what I feel for Raul.* She looked at him.

"He's handsome," she said aloud.

She dropped by his side and began to moan softly. Then the springs creaked. Raul turned slowly toward her and through her tears she saw him emerge from the heaviness of his sleep. She shuddered because she suddenly remembered the passage of Holy Writ she had read as a girl in boarding school, (when Lazarus returned from the world of shadows.) Without opening his eyes, Raul's arm raised up and grew like a strange and dark plant. The medal tinkled on his wrist and a fluttering came from the balcony. Sadness, in waves, grew, rolled away, and flooded with an increasing tide, isolating her from the world. A great coldness arrived. She felt frighteningly naked, spied upon by thousands and thousands of eyes. Other little girls, also naked and chubby cheeked, most of them plump, lay in the albums, exacerbating their childhood, stretched out like sad doll-like corpses, dressed—those of them that were—with their same deferred and indecent childhood, as her own mother—for different reasons—had forced her to dress. Dirty sailor dresses on small and round breasts of women. Raul's arm fell on her like an iron collar around her neck.

It was about four in the afternoon when Raul got up. He always got up without saying anything, like a stupid bull being born again from dark foam. He left and came back after a short while, dressed, with his temples dripping. She looked at him through half-closed eyelids. *I don't like him to wet his hair that way, when he plasters it down against his head.* She raised the sheet up to her chin.

"You've been prying into things there, huh?" he asked.

He came closer to the bed. She saw his long legs then looked up to his solid, square chin.

"Yes."

"And what do you think?"

"Nothing. What does it have to do with me, your nasty affairs? I'm not guilty of being Elena's daughter, I didn't choose anything of that."

Raul grabbed her chin and forced her to sit up in bed. He hurt her; she felt a sharp pain in her neck, in all of her body. But she didn't complain. She managed to smile and open her eyes, looking at him straight in the eye.

"You have chosen me," Raul said.

She let herself fall on her back. Through the cracks in the Venetian blinds the sun was already visibly coming in. The wind had stopped.)

"Until my mother discovered us."

Manuel was listening to her. She contemplated the sheen of his red hair, his hands folded together. He was almost a child. It pained her to talk to him, as if making a delayed confession. And, nevertheless she could not keep silent.

"Perhaps I'm bothering you, or boring you. I don't know why I'm telling you this."

Manuel's black eyes contrasted with his golden face. Something was born in him, strange and sad.

"Speak," he said. "Say whatever you want."

(The third day. She knew, from the time she awoke, that it was the third day. They had lived as in one long day. They ate sandwiches. Empty bottles were lined up under the desk. A heavy atmosphere of cigarette smoke, wrinkled papers and dusty wood, surrounded them. The bed appeared eternally unmade. On the small stool, on the tray, dirty cups were piling up next to the coffee pot. A fly, stupefied by the arrival of the cold, was milling around the edge of the sugar bowl. Wrapped up in Raul's bathrobe, she was looking at her feet against the stained carpet. Through the Venetian blind—still poorly fitting, never closed or open—arose an acrid smell of rotten fish and the voice of a woman screaming something in Basque. She liked to look at an engraving that hung over the desk. A man and a woman in wigs were swaying on a swing, while two too small ladies were whispering or reading something. Underneath the engraving she read, in neat English letters "Love on a swing." She ran her fingertip over the gilt frame. That could be, perhaps, Elena and the Milanese. What stupid and strange things the world brought with it inside its old belly.

In those days Raul heeded neither the telephone or any call at the door.

"I love you," he told her. "I want to be with you, I love you. Truly, I love you."

"The business is going to go under," she observed naively.

He began to laugh.

"Not here."

Raul's hands were pretty and dark. Perhaps what pleased her most was to feel his hands. It displeased her to see him eat. He would grab a sandwich, bring it up to his mouth and then his fangs would appear like enormous, bloodthirsty teeth.

"You look like a dog when you eat."

"I am a dog," he answered, chewing absently.

It was the third day. I knew it. *Something is going to happen.* I preferred to say nothing. Raul, lying down, was looking at the ceiling, his hands under the back of his neck. His cigarette was burning in his mouth, the smoke was coming out through his nose like a pair of thin and growing fangs. At that moment his vacant glance wandered toward the peeling ceiling from where the light cord was hanging down like a row of dead insects.

"You like silk, the way a woman does," she said, stroking his body.

"The way a prostitute does," corrected Raul.

And, at that moment, someone violently shook the door. The key trembled, with its thin, metal tag carrying the same number, 23—23, just exactly as at the table of the first night at the Casa de los Negroes. The tag and key suddenly seemed like his bracelet with its fearful cabalistic sign. A righteous fist, exasperated, pounded on the door, once, twice, three times. *The number three pursues me*, she said to herself. She drew back and bumped into the small stool. The cups rattled, a spoon, with heavy a drop of coffee, fell to the floor. Raul's hand, which held the cigarette, remained fixed in the air.

"Hide in the bathroom." Raul's voice, like an exasperating lizard, advanced over a vast velvet world.

"I don't feel like it," she answered.

The door clattered like a ship's prow. Raul advanced slowly and opened the door. Because of that violence it just seemed that the door was going to tumble down on him. But, instead, a pale and wrinkled ghost appeared, leaning as though fainting, on the door frame. *But you haven't dyed the roots*, she thought, seeing her advance slowly, the washed out curls on each side of her face like a wig. Not even her own hair seemed to belong to her. *It's strange, in order for her to be truly herself, she would have to scrub herself with a washcloth, pull out her hair, eyebrows, eyelashes, to leave herself without eyelids, naked*, like that mistreated celluloid doll that they bought for her once, and from which she stripped everything. Finally she cut it open from top to bottom with a kitchen paring-knife. Inside she found only a kind of pink-colored bellows that, upon being pressed between her fingers, said, "mama!" like a meowing sound.)

9

Perhaps what will surprise you the most is that my mother was very religious. She never gave up going to Mass. Every Sunday she would ask me, "Have you been to Mass? Yes or no? Tell me the truth." She wanted to know if I had been to confession, she advised me to get a Father Confessor. She used to say to me, "Only that will save you." I know it very well. She had a statue of the Virgin in her sitting-room, with velvet roses and little golden candlesticks. When I was a very little girl she made me kneel every night and pray before going to bed. And my first Communion! It was something fantastic. I was vomiting all night from all the cakes and cookies I had eaten.

("Yours is the worst one in the world," said Elena. "It's a sin that no priest can pardon, miserable girl, miserable girl."

She said it in a terrible voice, like the meowing bellows squeezed by the innocent hands of a five year old girl. She entered the room, like the fog in the woods, something diffuse and which, nevertheless, covers everything. She remained next to the tray with its dirty cups, with the remains of the sugar and coffee, and tears fell on both sides of her mother's mouth, following again the little ruts of wrinkled age, spreading out in the furrows of her mouth, in a way that repelled.

"Look, let's not talk about sins. Don't come to me with those things that leave me cold. You're a living sin. At least I'm a natural being, because this man is closer to me in age."

The gold cross shone on Elena's chest and her long finger pointed it out.

"Look! He had compassion and you forget that compassion is the only thing that can save us."

Suddenly, in the middle of the fog, she wanted to understand her.

"I would like to be able to understand the situation, but you have never had sympathy for anyone but yourself. It doesn't matter in any case."

Her eyes of a soft and terrible gold, like two enormous muscatel grapes on which the rain might have remained, were fixed on her, with a pain so remote, or evasive, that she felt uneasy.

"You are more miserable than I," Elena said.

Up to that moment Raul appeared not to exist. But suddenly he stepped up.

"Elena, my dear, my love.")
"I went away with him."
(Her voice emerged from some barrier one can not come back from.) Manuel leaned over toward her and took her hand, small and dirty, evasive. He held it between his, pensively.

"Do you know something? There was something in Jeza, like a thread, that tied us together and kept on returning to itself."

"I always thought that of him, although not in those words," Marta said.

Once more there was a joy, almost repressed, in her words. (When speaking of Jeza she seemed to wake up from something, from some dark fog in which she argued with herself and from which she wished to escape.) For him, too, Jeza was something that he should approach, like a blind sailboat across a dark sea that raises up incessant and powerful waves, turbulent black waves.

"In one way or another I have the impression that Jeza leads us where he wants," she said.

Marta went toward the lamp, stretched out her hand, put it over the light where it remained light and transparent. Something was alive and sure among the drifts of fog that surrounded them. She turned around to look at him and smiled.

"And as for you, what linked you to him? When I received your first letter, believe me Manuel, I scarcely remembered you."

"I was almost a boy when I met him. I also have a very hazy remembrance of you. I remembered your eyes."

(It is Jeza's death the unites us. Death can be something so alive, concrete and sure like existence.)

"Why did you see him again?"

"Es Mariné told me what happened to Simeón and Zacarias...and that he was still in prison. I supposed that you would like me to see him since his letters didn't reach you and yours didn't reach him."

"But, why, Manual? Your life has changed, everything is different. You're no longer the little boy that I met."

"Because I needed it," said Manuel.

In his voice was something hurting which moved her. She put her hand on his head and stroked his hair. He looked at the floor, as though he didn't dare raise his eyes.

"Everything has fallen to pieces; uprightness, desire for goodness, hope. I need to recover something I'd lost. And I am afraid as though I were at the edge of the abyss and something, someone was pushing toward the bottom."

"I, too, am afraid," she said. She scarcely said so, but he heard it. (When I met Jeza everything changed. To the point that at that moment everything was empty, mean and sad. I was enamored of life, but I knew nothing of life. That was the best thing about Jeza: discovering life for me. I don't know whether he could be mistaken. Suddenly everything changed meaning. Jeza was not a ghost. Up to then everything to me seemed like tracks in the sand, like the echo of footsteps.)

"Jeza was, in himself, an affirmation," he said. The fact that he might be mistaken didn't enter into my calculations."

Manuel was silent. He couldn't share anything with her, neither memories nor childhood, not even an idea of the world (a subtle fabric, like a spider's web, is being woven silently out of the darkness in order not to separate us, for some mysterious reason that I don't know even how to explain, even to myself.)

"I lived through that time. When they used to get together in the abandoned house. Jose Taronji, Simeón and Zacarias. And now Es Mariné doesn't want to say anything to me. He's afraid. Everybody's afraid, Marta."

Fear is the silence of the islands, in the broad, blue sea, reflecting like a mirror, fear is the silence of the streets and the dust and the sand raised by the wind. Fear is the Port, like a motionless sea, a turbulent and slow mirror, green and mute under the afternoon sky, where the sea breaks against and splashes the porcelain balustrades. Fear is an enormous funnel, whirled about like the sea, that devours the boats. I'm afraid, and Es Mariné and Jocobo and Jose Taronji and Marta are afraid, we are all afraid, we will always live in fear.

"No," he screamed submissively.

She looked at him, frightened.

"We have to get out of this," he said. "I don't want to! I can't do it!"

Marta agreed, but perhaps she didn't hear. He guessed that she didn't hear him. In spite of everything she stretched her hand out to him. Then she realized the simplicity, almost the innocence, of those eyes.

(Inasmuch as I was afraid when I left the funeral and went to the woods where Jose Taronji was buried, inasmuch as I was afraid and everything was a search for reasons, or facts, that justified something. I felt cowardice in front of my mother and my brothers, because they were hungry, and I felt cowardice in front of this house which, in spite of everything, I loved so much as well as my childhood which was already struggling like a bird. Inasmuch as I wanted to flee from Jorge de Son Major, one day I went to see Jeza.)

Fog

A Man Called Jeza

The war was coming to an end. A thick fog was floating over the Port and surveillance of the coast was letting up. Voices appeared in the fog, remote calls. Christmas had passed, but some children were still running through the alleys of the Port with the same old songs. Their footsteps split away from the silence and fell, like other echoes, other voices.

It was the twelfth of August,1939, at five-thirty in the afternoon. It was practically night. Jeza's wife and a baby boy left the island in a motor boat. The fog and the bad weather helped them. At dawn they made out the wall of the Garraf. Near Castelldefels a patrol boat stopped them and they were taken to the Commandant of the Navy. After half-an-hour two agents of the SIM arrived. The woman made herself known and requested contact with Esteban Martin, a member of the Regional Committee of the Party. She handed over the documents and they were released.

1

"Don't get me involved," said Es Mariné. "Leave me in peace."
Manuel drew close to the balustrade, and Sanamo followed him, running around like a puppy.

"The boat is down there below. Lately he used to go out in her; although the boats are controlled and nobody can have it without the knowledge of the authorities…that's the way he was. As you already know."

Sanamo took something from his pocket and brought it to his ear. Manuel recognized it immediately. It was Jorge de Son Major's watch. Also his overcoat, the frayed and coveted overcoat with its velvety collar that the old man almost dragged along, getting it entangled in the coils of rope, shaking it out with loving care, as he had seen ladies do.

"The sea, Manuelito," said Sanamo. "Do you remember? When we went out together to the sea, with him… Do you remember? The sea of the Greeks and the Phoenicians…"

(Through the sea of the heroes and the dealers, the unfolded sail of the sun flees, rosy and cruel, toward its death. Jorge de Son Major's old watch, with its blue enamel work, is a great incentive, too. Everything pushes on, everything revolves, like the sun and the thunder, over the sea. The old, stopped watch that Sanamo is shaking at his ear, as though he were pretending to wake up some lazy little animal by repeating the voice of a dead time. Sanamo and Es Mariné are afraid. Nobody wants to let himself be imprisoned by something he doesn't want. But the watch at his ear shouts in its silence and Sanamo shakes it at his ear, hoping not to die too soon.)

"Do you happen to see her?" mumbled Sanamo. His lips were trembling.

"Scarecrow," exclaimed Es Mariné. "Take off those clothes if you want to come to this house. Cursed raven, you don't respect anything." Es Mariné's burning eye fastened on Sanamo's right hand where the watch was shining. Sanamo hid it at the bottom of his pocket.

"You have always envied me," he said. "I know that already. I swear to you that he would not have stepped a foot in your house if not for this angel…an angel come down from heaven."

"I don't want to know anything," repeated Es Mariné. "Nothing. Leave me in peace."

He turned his back on them and entered the house.

"Let's go"

The staircase to the landing started out to the right of the terrace. Sanamo preceded him. His little knobby hand clutched the edge of the banister. He stepped carefully so he wouldn't trip.

The Antinea was a typical Mollorcan boat with a motor. Under the arches of Es Mariné's terrace the water gave off an obscure echo, like a restrained scream. He heard the beat of the waves against the piles of pink stone. The Antinea appeared, moored, like a noble animal.

"You are how old now?"

Manuel hesitated for a moment.

"I'm going to be nineteen."

"But you're really a child." And he thought (that's not the way it is, you should say, I'm never going to be nineteen.) She said it in a very low voice so that Manuel wouldn't hear her.

A low and grey wind rose up and swept away the fog.

"If we are lucky", said Manuel, "we would have the fog with us. (If we are lucky we will be able to die on time.) A pain, a great remorse, an ill-adapted version of youth arose between the two of them.

"I don't want to drag you away from all this, Manuel. Leave me alone. You have done enough for Jeza and me."

He didn't seem to hear her.

"Surveillance of the coast is practically non-existent," he informed her. (Es Mariné had said, "The war is won, but, in any case, be careful. The best time is five-thirty, six... As for me, leave me in peace. I don't know anything. Don't get me involved.)

There was a word between them that they didn't want to say at any cost. A blind word of silence floating around. (Everything seems to indicate that a mission will be carried out or, perhaps, a hope.) Something that could gain something for someone, something beneficial.

Es Mariné said, "Good luck. I wish both of you good luck."

(Animals never make useless gestures, only men do. But we do only what we can do, nobody is a hero for nothing, we learn a few figures, mistaken or not, and then we die.)

"The motor is in good shape."

Sanamo appeared—he had been with them for a while and, nevertheless, up to that moment, he hadn't been seen or heard—and screeched.

"In perfect condition. The gentlemen would often go out with me. We took a little cruise. Only for the sake of remembering." Marta trembled. (*Only for the sake of remembering.* This is the way old men do it. I am going to explore the death of my life, my own death. Jeza, Jeza, what did you do with me. But, unlike so much talking about you and to you, we don't let you say anything. Unlike us, poor pawns suitable for the big trap. Your life, your death, is more eloquent than all the words that can be said. I now have a strange feeling that Jeza never existed, that he is a pure invention on our part. José Taronji, me, Manuel, Raul from his angle... Yes, we have invented him. Nobody will know, really, who he was, what he thought, what contradictions he had to endure inside his heavy shell of a man. I know what Jeza did, I don't know either what he felt or what he thought. Against what inner feelings he had to struggle, against what doubts, against what fears. I'll never know it. It belongs to him, as does death.) She was cold and she wrapped herself up in her jacket. Through the window she saw the fog escaping. Tiny little mirrors were forming on the ground, shining. She turned to Sanamo.

"Can I ask you something?"

"Go ahead." The old man looked at her with disturbed little eyes. (To the contrary of Es Mariné, faithful to an idea, to a feeling, Sanamo had been born, perhaps, to betray his own reasons. He benefits from the hidden, the clandestine. Clear things don't suit him. His guitar, perhaps, will always hang nostalgically from the nail. He doesn't wear roses in his ear.)

"Go sometime to my little son's and ask Marcela to forgive me."

"Do you have a little son, dove?" Sanamo murmured. "I didn't know that. Believe me. I didn't know."

"He's up there with Simeón's sister. Yes, you know her. I know that you know her."

"I'm not from around here, lamb. I'm not acquainted with anyone. I was born far away from here."

Manuel put a hand on her shoulder.

"Let's go," he said. (A cutting edge cuts, suddenly, all the fastenings, the troubled ties that a human being weaves with the earth, ships that don't want to leave.)

"Then I cannot entrust him to anyone?" she insisted.

"To no one, that's certain," said Sanamo. "That's very certain. But, how about a glass of wine?"

Manuel blinked. (A voice, here, said, *you will remember in the last moment some dark roses, those drops of rain.* Everything becomes undone and falls like dust. That was not true.)

"Let's have that wine, Sanamo. For you. For your long years of life."

"Yes," shouted the old man.

He had suddenly become excited, he raised himself on the tips of his feet, brandishing his twisted and dark finger.

"I'll live, I'll live for a long time, young man, ungrateful son. I'll live for a long time so that my tongue gets tired of cursing you."

And he began to cry. His flood of tears, like a dry rain, made one smile rather than anything else. Manuel put his hand on his head.

"I am not sure of what you say. Calm down."

He almost felt like drying his tears and blowing his nose the way one does for a small boy. Sanamo rubbed his wet cheeks.

"That's the way it is, Manuel, ungrateful boy. I'll live for a long time. I'll sing your little song and I'll say: Listen, it's the story of an unfortunate little boy that went to lose his war. It will seem something unusual to many people. You always were. At times I thought you were the living incarnation of the Other One. Alas, little red-haired fellow, how sad it is to be with you."

He put his hand on his head and added, "It seems that those curls are going to be on fire from one moment to the other. You're like a flame, you can set a whole forest on fire."

"Enough," said Manuel. "You have read too many stories."

"Your father knew it! Your father who poisoned my life, he knew it. He taught me to read at twenty-seven, but, cursed be my fate, for so much evil."

(He will live for a long time and his life will be the worst punishment. He wants to die and he doesn't know how. We are lucky after all.)

Outside, as the fog fled, the cold took possession of everything.

2

It was a clean and orderly attic where someone had cleaned, one by one, all the broken objects...lanterns, tiny sailboats, Greek and Phoenician ships. It was Jorge de Son Major's sitting room, deprived of liberty and blind, holding the lament of the objects.

"Give me the sack, Sanamo," said Manuel.

The seaman's bag crawled and moved forward across the floor with a velvety friction, like the belly of an animal.

"The compass, the telescopes, the naval maps," prayed Sanamo like a litany, lining up the objects on Jorge de Son Major's table. He had waxed and polished the table and it smelled like a honeycomb.

"Sanamo, is it here that you found him dead?"

"Definitely. Here."

"How was it, Sanamo? Did you realize immediately what had happened?"

"Oh, no! Not immediately. I was going to the kitchen. I had prepared lamb with mint, the way he liked it. I was going to tell him. I went upstairs and called twice at the door and he didn't answer. But he was in the habit of doing that at times, and I understood that he wanted to be alone, not speak to anyone. I went downstairs again. I was fidgeting with my things. You know I'm very careful with my things, this house was always the mirror of my heart... Then the hour struck by the clock, and thus, without more ado, my heart turned over, a striking of the bell, just as I'm telling you. And I said to myself, "Ay, Sanamo, Sanamo, the Lord is abandoning you."

"Which one of them? How many masters do you serve?"

"Don't be naughty, little one. You aren't like you used to be. You're not the boy I loved so much... that he loved so much, when he used to say to me, 'How did I, a crow, beget such a dove?'"

"Be still, Sanamo, he never managed to speak the way you do. With you, one can never know anything for certain."

"Don't get angry. Listen, follow the thread of the story. I came in and there he was, bent over the table. He seemed to be asleep. But when I gave him a thump on the shoulder, he sank down toward the right and fell like a sack. Poor *señor*, his heart was wasted away. Because, boy, the insides, like machines, wear away, spoil, get obstructed, for some dumb reason or another. Well, that's the way it is, it can't be helped. People die every day, of something or another. The doctor said it was angina of the chest. I cried a great deal, I swear to you. There were roses everywhere, red, the way he liked them. I went and brought some, it was all I was able to. I threw them on top of him and said to myself, it's the last thing I can do for you, because you'll never hear my poor guitar again.... Do you believe, Manuel, that he'll never hear it again? And you, Manuel, will you hear it sometimes? It will be very sad to think that, soon, if you want to remember something, you will have to go and look for the cawings of that old vulture of Es Mariné... Only he, in spite of everything, will hear the guitar with the same ears as my *señor*, or you, my child. Do you remember, do you remember?" Suddenly he became weak, his hands fell, the going to and fro (with which he tried to help pick up and hold objects) was abandoned. He was silent as if he thought nobody was going to hear his string of words, his songs (now that his whole life, too, is stripped and falls around him.)

"Death destroys you, old man possessed by the devil," said Manuel, with the affection that still came from the more and more distant shore of his childhood.

"I'll live, Manuel, I'll live. I'll bury Es Mariné. I swear it." He made a cross with his index finger and thumb and kissed it.

Suddenly an idea floated in his little eyes.

"Listen, Manuelito, little one. Have you made a will? Have you remembered me?"

On the twelfth of January, about seven in the morning, it began to rain. At two-thirty the rain stopped and a weak sun grew pale over objects. Then an obscure strip advanced over the sea, low clouds withdrew to the east, and the sky was changed onto a broad swollen canvas. The wind blew against invisible sails and legions of seagulls descended to the edge of the beach, screaming. On Es Mariné's terrace Marta was contemplating the flight of the clouds and the wind.

"Take this," said Es Mariné.

He held something out to her, but she only looked at him, strangely like a ghost, among the empty cages. Mambrú turned its inflamed eyes. In a short time Es Mariné's hair had turned completely white. He had grown completely old.

"It's the only thing that I can give you, my farewell gift."

She took the bottle in silence.

"Here they come," said Es Mariné.

She ran to the balustrade, leaned her waist on it, and peered at the water. The night poured itself, placed itself between the light and the world. Sanamo's small boat drew near.

"Let's go," said Es Mariné.

It was approximately five-fifteen. They went down the staircase to the small landing. Manuel unloaded the sack. Sanamo was quiet against the piling. Jorge de Son Major's overcoat almost grazed his shoes and with delight he stroked the facings of the faded velvet.

"Nobody fears anything now," said Es Mariné.

Manuel untied the Antinea. Es Mariné went up to him, clutched his arm, turned toward himself and sought, with a mute despair, his face, his eyes.

"Once I helped to betray you without knowing it. I want to say one thing to you. Have you forgiven me?"

"There's nothing to forgive," said Manuel. That seemed to exasperate Es Mariné.

"You're mad."

Marta noticed that something, something hidden and already lost in a time that could not be returned to, trembled in his voice. (A voice when, perhaps, he desired, lived, or had been able to die for something.)

"You're mad, both of you," she repeated. (A hand which had been grasping something for years and, suddenly, had to let go and abandon its object; shamelessly contracted, holding the void, the silence.)

"Leave them in peace now!" Sanamo cried. "Perhaps you think they're going to pay attention to you? Leave them alone, they belong to another race. Perhaps they might get lucky."

"Not the luck that you and I can know," said Es Mariné sternly.

The two old men were now very close, their two silhouettes stood out against the dark sea. Night had already arrived. Sanamo's hand, a fist of vine roots, continued stroking the black velvet, a hand (a grey spider where life revolves agonizingly, a hand attached to the world, to the smoothness of dull velvet, life, like death, opens a path with blows there, alongside there, in his toothless mouth in his little eyes of a household devil), more and more weak and dull. (I do not love this life, I can not love it if they don't show me something better, beyond where I was. I don't understand life because my life expected something different. On our backs remain the masters of the earth, passive women, curious and defenseless children like animals, all of them, losing one by one the minutes of life, like the drops of a splendid and poisonous liquid. Death can be something complete, sensual.) Manuel looked at the girl. Her hair, smooth and golden, fell behind her ears. She looked like a boy. (She never looked like a woman to me because, in spite of her beauty, there was something separating her, something different.)

He helped her jump onto the Antinea. It was growing dark. A few minutes before he could scarcely make out their faces. Not now. Es Mariné carried a lantern in his hand but had not lit it. Over the sea the fog was becoming thick again. The waves beat against the sides of the Antinea. The strip of silver that sparkled over the Ensenada de Santa Catalina, where they had killed José Taronji, had also disappeared in the fog and the night. He threw the sack over the gunholds and fell back (like someone throwing food into the cellar of someone infected by the plague.)

"I've put in food. A lot of food, Manuelito, flavored with mint. May God keep you," he cut short suddenly.

His voice had the still and passionate spluttering of logs, of leaves piled up in bonfires, in Son Major's garden. A silence had just been born (but the deepest silence is here, in this corner, in the compact mass of his shadow. Es Mariné's silence originates in voices, distant, lost, echoes of some chorus that explains what has to be done in order to live, in order to breathe, to drink and walk on the earth, with heavy burdens on one's back and conscience. Ashes that the wind hurls over an implacable sand; the whole island, suddenly, seems to be entered there, in its darkness and in its human silence.)

"Mariné," he called in a scarcely audible voice.

But Es Mariné did not answer and seemed to sink even more into the darkness It was Sanamo who said, with a muffled cry (it is to himself that he is saying good bye, it is to himself that he is crying, it is himself that he is burying and whose body he is covering with roses and tears.)

"Good bye, my life, good bye. May heaven keep you and may all the gods which exist or which may exist or might have existed, accompany you to wherever you are going... *good bye, prince of my house, my child.*

His voice, more than being heard, was guessed at (because I have heard these words and this voice so many times that perhaps I am only thinking it, it is I who hears his thought. He asked me whether I'd listen to the music of his guitar sometime) and the silence was something overcome (infinitely irreversible; a row of bare trees, black in the night; the echo of a lose anvil; ashes, corpses burned and strewn about, being lashed by the wind. In all this blackness, in the shadow of Es Mariné's quiet body, a great complaint; a slow requiem, like the hidden voice of the world, approximating a twilight out of time. There is no yesterday or today, only a long, white defenseless region, without land or stream where howl the cries of men who ask for rain, of the women who ask for love, of children who raise useless scales of justice, where good and evil do not maintain their balance. The world here, now, loses its dimensions and something, an enormous tongue perhaps, runs across the earth damply. The broad tongue of hunger and thirst.)

The Antinea was waiting. Manuel bent over in the darkness and the motor began to sputter. Something moved Sanamo, perhaps he wanted to say something. He drew near to the edge of the sea and raised his two hands. But his voice became lost, his hissing was already a memory and the earth was already bidding good-bye to both of them (the entire island, with its white gardenias, and the Resurrection from the dead bids good-bye, with a hand that relaxes its pressure). With scarcely a sensation of movement the Antinea went forward through a course that, although recently begun, was effaced (like the track of a step of someone who is no longer there, who perhaps did not exist anymore.)

3

The first one who climbed up the stairs was Es Mariné. Sanamo followed him. Once inside the house he turned on the light. A dirty light-bulb was hanging from a cord covered with flies. In the yellowish light objects took on shape, the boxes of canned goods with their brands of broth, the heaps of soap, the jam and pickles, the little boxes of cinnamon, saffron and clove, the bottles. The heavy odor of the spices filled the atmosphere. He turned around.

"Are you there?"

"Yes," answered Sanamo.

It was cold, They could hear the quick running back and forth of the rats. Something clinked.

"What's that?"

"I don't know."

"Well, let's have a drink."

"Yes. A long time ago, a very long time ago, Mariné, I would have come to tell you something. You know I have always spoken ill of you, but at the bottom of my heart...."

"Shut up! Don't come to me with your gibberish!"

An arm was groping in the dark, a flat hand, with short hairy fingers, looking for the black belly of the bottle on the shelf. The rats were scampering back and forth between the cartons, accustomed to the scant light. The fog stuck to the window pane like a breath.

"I don't know whether you remember this liqueur," said Es Mariné. "I kept it for a while and I said to myself, one day someone will come who will drink it and pay. Mytelena. Andros...."

Sanamo raised both his hands and covered his face.

"Don't whine. Look at me. I don't know what that is."

He poured the liquid into two blue glasses (so blue, all of a sudden), in the dark enclosure, with its vapor of merchandise, of rancid candy, dark powders of dream.

"Sanamo, Sanamo," Es Mariné said slowly, clicking his tongue against his palate. We have never liked each other, and now..."

"This is hell," groaned the other, while wiping his lips clean with the back of his hand. "I read about it once. This is it. You know, old octopus, we never liked each other. And now if we want to have something of what we loved (just something, I said, eh?) we'll have to pry about each other in order to find it."

"Look, stop your string of words with me. I don't have his patience."

His patience, like a bird with its head cut off, fell at once between the two of them.

"You're not even worth crying about," Sanamo said. "Come on, pour me another drink. In Mytilena I used to cry and you'd make fun of me. I really did have a heart, filthy old man, I really did have a heart."

"Your little boys knew," laughed Es Mariné. "Ah, Sanamo, Sanamo, to think that it makes me happy to have you here now. Truly, we're old, death is so close!"

"To yours, idiot," said Sanamo. He chugged his drink in one swallow. "If I had the power, as, for example, Taronji had," Sanamo's eyes shone, saturated with the sweet, sad liqueur, "I would have dragged the corpse to the center of the square, and all the gentlemen (the true gentlemen of Sa Jorge) would have galloped in a circle, on black horses, screaming, before burying him. That would have been his real funeral, while here....ah, Mariné, Mariné, what a sad time has fallen for us to endure."

"Imbecile," said Es Mariné, filling up the glasses again.

"But I'm only a servant."

"And as for me, I'm a sailor. There you have the difference. I have never humbled myself, nor will I ever humble myself."

"And I'm a poet," continued Sanamo. "He said it. Only you and whores are still poets."

"Curse you, will you give up talking this way? Don't you realize what's going on? Don't you have guts, you old faggot? Don't you have any brains under that scouring pad?"

He suddenly became infuriated, went toward a corner, and in his hands carried something long, green and shining.

"Look what I do with everything. Look what I do with everything that binds us together."

He raised his two hands which held the bottle with the reproduction of the Delfín.

"No, Mariné, no!" Sanamo tried to stop him, but it was too late. Mariné threw it to the ground and stepped on it. The thin wood shavings, the paper sails, the shells piled up in the bottom of the bottle, creaked under his boots. Sanamo remained fearful, his mouth falling down, like a clown's.

"Why do you do that?"

"And perhaps he wouldn't set fire to it one day?"

"That's different. We don't have anything else."

"We don't have anything else? We don't have anything else because we don't deserve it. We're merchants, Sanamo, merchants we will die."

"Come on, Sanamo, lift up the bottle and the glasses. Let's drink a little. Do you want to smoke?"

"You don't have what I like to smoke."

"Not now, Sanamo."

The rats were gnawing at the candles and at the bars of soap.

"I have the other Delfin at home. Identical with the one you just broke, I don't think everyone dies." Sanamo swallowed a hiccup.

There was no moon, only fog, somewhat fleeing. The same fog that used to surround the murmuring of the Antinea, which even now was crackling in their ears.

And the night grew deeper. Es Mariné remained asleep, against the table. Sanamo held off for a while longer, and finally fell down between the coils of rope, crossing the velvet collar over his chest.

When the sun came out, a scream from Mambrú got Es Mariné up in one jump. He rubbed his eyes hard. The fog still covered everything. The lamp bulb that was still on, was an eye, round and yellow, full of dust. And all the advertisements for beer, soup, coffees, spices, wines, soaps and chocolates shook under a polished light.

"Sanamo," said Es Mariné quietly. "Sanamo, wake up and leave. Dawn is breaking."

A glow, like a watchful glance, invaded her field of vision; the pale sky cut across by the dark stiffness of the water. Then, something opened up, like a wide, silvery path, and the strip of water revived, incessantly. It was getting to be dawn.

The waves came in interminable battalions, curling up, weakening and dying, striking against the hull in a soft and doughy fashion. The Antinea went up and fell down, tugging at her lines. It seemed to wake up, shake, return, little by little and hold back for a moment, like a swimmer among the waves, throwing itself forward. It shifted, threw itself on one side, and fell on the depths of the waves. Then she realized what was going on.

Everything, up to that moment, was like a lethargic sleep, like a fog, or a curtain of smoke. But now they were there, getting inexorably close to the coast. From out of the fog the outline of the mass of rocks began to be seen.

A patrol boat was approaching, showing its silhouette little by little in the fog. They heard the voices from up above. The coast rose up, closer, amid the transparent and blue smoke. Suddenly, when she heard the men's voices, Marta recognized the silence that had held them during the night. (We haven't said a single word since we left.) Each one of them was closed up in his own silence. (Perhaps the poor boy has been afraid.) She had dozed a little. He hadn't. They had worked together, experienced together the coveted emotion, their fear almost. She didn't know whether he had been afraid. She wasn't able to figure it out, in that great anxiety that unfolded in her since Jeza's death.

Eight men manned the boat. The machine guns shone in the emerging light. Marta looked at the men. Three were too old, five too young, almost children (that gives the measure of things). But she didn't feel any weakness

The port was showing its outline, like an ancient and almost forgotten ghost. It was a strange cemetery where the first effect of the sun and the fog floated. The hulls of various sunken vessels emerged from the water. Enormous, shifting corpses paraded slowly before her eyes, bodies sleeping in the black water, with human, dense death.

The sailors inspected the Antinea. One of the boys opened the sack of food Sanamo had carefully prepared. Avid hands searched diligently, divided up the food, almost with ferocity, bespattered by the foam, the fog, the weak light of the dawn. With one arm he held fast his weapon, the other held a piece of chewed meat raised toward his mouth. The machine guns had an almost painful blackness. They split the food into little portions and passed them around. Their words, the shine of their eyes and their weapons, had a distant, strange clicking sound in the dawn. Only the sunken boats gave a dimension of mute tragedy.

They disembarked, lead by the sailors. Two of them remained on the Antinea which had been tied up. The fog was dispersing there, like a fleeing, golden fog.

"Everything in ruins," murmured Marta. Manuel turned his head and smiled at her. He didn't know what she felt, he had never seen it, he wasn't able to feel it. The blackish buildings, the burnt deposits of oil, the sheds half-fallen down, their upper roofs with holes in them. All the facades seemed to be stripped of plaster by the machine-guns. *He's not able to feel what I feel.*

4

There was a little chalet next to the curve of the highway, between the damp grass of the vacant lots. The small, pink house, with its low windows had a mossy iron railing, the house, rising up. The house was real, terribly certain, empty.

"What are you going to do? Don't you see that everything is lost? Everything is over here. Come with us. We'll make a place for you in the car, I promise you. Come, much can still be done, away from here. Here, no."

Esteban Martin was a short, broad man, with thick grey hair. His china-blue eyes looked at her with a mixture of compassion and astonishment.

"Nobody is left here now" she said.

With a gesture, Esteban Martin pointed out the house.

"Look at it. No one. Believe me, come, we're on time. Let's go to France. Cars are scarce, but you should come with me. Come."

Esteban's impatient hand was on her shoulder.

A cloud of black, black particles in the air came toward them. In the garden of the house, papers, flies and letters were burning. Small fires invaded the still damp earth and, at that moment, she felt an immense pain in the throat, as if they had nailed minute and sharp pieces of glass in her throat.

"Manuel," she said.

The boy, silent and pensive, followed at her side. What boy saw him now, with his head turned sideways, his eyes clouded over, looking toward the ground.

"Manuel, you go with them."

Manuel didn't say anything.

They went in. Two men were still piling up papers. Esteban stepped aside and went to speak with them. A torn poster, dragged by the end, rolled toward their feet. Marta bent over and picked it up. It was a piece of paper with a soldier on it. Discolored by the sun and the rain, it shook between her fingers. The smoke, the soot came near them again.

"I lived here with Jeza," said Marta.

At seven in the evening, the January wind did not stir up a single noise in the corners, not a sound of the sweeping wind, not even the wind itself was heard. It wasn't cold, only an increasing dampness soaked the walls and the earth. From the garden shadows were born under the bare trees. Through the window pane the night sky was turning silver.

"Why haven't you gone with them?" asked Marta.

He was there, in the frame of the door. He didn't say anything, he only looked at her, silently, with a tranquility that gave something back to him. An echo, lost or forgotten, an interior time, that had nothing to do with the clock.

(Raul had big, white teeth, shining between coarse lips. When he laughed his eyes became strangely small, they almost closed in the blackened face, from all of him emanated something ferocious and handsome. He laughed.

"Well, girl, the comedy is finished," he said. "Do you think you're capable of following me?"

She had been waiting for him for a day and a half. He went with Elena on the day she discovered them. Now he returned, he was there, smiling, not laughing.

"Fine, I'll give it a try," she said. I don't have anything to lose."

Raul put his arms around her shoulders. She noted his hand on her neck.

"Has she died?"

Raul pressed his hand deeper against her throat.

"What pleases me most about you," he said, "is that you don't have a conscience. Let's get away from here, this place stinks, I'm drowning. Let's go to Barcelona, I have good friends there. Everything will be all right."

"I believe it."

But she didn't believe it, nor did she give up believing it. It made no difference to her. The situation was, as he had said, *this place stinks, I'm suffocating*.)

"I'm staying with you," said Manuel.

"You should've gone away with them. You shouldn't have stayed."

Manuel went to the fireplace, which had burned out. He stooped down, crumpled a handful of paper, grabbed a fistful of chips and set the paper on fire.

"There is a little wood that's still left downstairs. Esteban left cans of food and something to eat."

He smiled for the first time since a long time. He looked juvenile, almost happy, stooping over like this. Marta contemplated his dark hands that had already caught her attention because of their strength. Hands, like everything else about him, gave the impression of violent, savage strength, held in like a scream. He was a tall and powerful boy; and for that reason the gentle tension that was evident in all his gestures was all the more surprising. Something like a howl that he held in, that he didn't want, by any means, to let escape from his throat, from his total being.

The house had been stripped of glass, curtains, draperies, and shutters. The windows appeared bare, horribly open, like eyes without eyelids. She went to the basement in search of wood and brought some up. Manuel was still stooping in front of the fireplace. The fire lit up and rose into the black and cold opening. The window panes reflected like mirrors and the few pieces of furniture that remained took on a halo of pink heat. She sat down beside him, looking at the fire.

(The first of October they arrived at the city, when it was growing dark in Raul's Panhard. They settled down in a boarding house in the Calle Mayor de Gracia, near the Rambla del Prat. The room had a balcony that looked out on the Calle Mayor. Raul opened the window wide and the blinds pounded violently against the wall. With his open hand he pointed out the facade of the building cross the way. He drew her near him; she noticed the arm pressing around her shoulders. Something strange, unknown, was upsetting him.

"Look, there it is," he said.

"What?"

"There, opposite, that shop, the cleaning supplies store."

She saw a wide door, with a window on each side. She could read a red sign. Viuda de Pablo Zarco (Pablo Zarco's widow), cleaning supplies.

"There it is, my childhood," he said smiling. But something muffled engulfed that laugh. Perhaps he hates this childhood as I do.

"There?"

"There, you don't think it's true, do you? Then look, do you see that window, in the upper part of the house? That one, toward the left, tall and narrow. I spent many nights there, exhausted, worn-out, awake."

She didn't know what to say. Everything seemed foreign and strange to her and the passion in Raul's voice bothered her. *I don't want them to confide in me,* she said to herself. *I don't like people to tell me their dirty stories. Nor do I share my stories with anyone. That's for Dionisia, Elena, and people like that. As for me, let them leave me alone.* She shook his arm free from her shoulders and began to unpack the suitcase. She observed him out of the corner of her eye. He turned his back to her, his arms crossed over his chest, looking at the street. They began to light the street lamps and a greenish brightness extended through the sky and entered the room. Irritated, she turned on the light.

"Close the blinds. It's cold."

Raul obeyed, in silence.

"I never spoke to you about my brother, did I?" He said unexpectedly.

"No."

"We used to work together, over there. It was so long ago and, yet now all of that appears as though it were only a few days ago.... As if it were yesterday."

"Fine."

"It doesn't make any difference to you, does it?"

She shrugged her shoulders.

It happened a few days later. It was in the early hours of the morning, when she was sleeping and heard hurried steps, the noise in the street, the screams. She opened her eyes, startled. Raul was on the balcony, peeping over, with his two arms leaning on the small iron railing.

"What's going on?" she asked, jumping out of her bed. Her eyelids were still half-closed. She came up close behind him and looked over his shoulder. Down there, in the street, several men, dressed in strange beige-colored uniforms with straps, were raising the paving stones from the street and making a kind of wall with them.

"What are they doing?"

"They're setting up a barricade," said Raul. His voice sounded strange to her and she looked at him curiously. He bit his lip, his eyes were half-closed. *He looks like that when he is envious or wants something badly.*

Throughout the entire day the street was a seething crowd.
"Don't go out of the house," Raul said.

The proprietor of the boarding house, a fat woman with very
black hair and eyelids painted blue, spoke precipitously through the
partition. A loudspeaker was whining. It filled the street. And the
radio, turned on at full volume by the landlady, filled the house with
a loud noise. The guests were gathered together in the small dining
room. Everybody seemed nervous. Two of the guests were fighting.
She heard their screams, their insults. Raul poked his head through the
door.

"Don't be frightened," he said. "And don't leave the room."

"I'm not frightened, what do these people mean to me?" she said.
"I don't understand what's going on or what they're saying."

"They're speaking in Catalan. But, in any case, whatever language they were speaking in, you wouldn't understand anything
anyhow. You're lucky."

A yellow flag, with red stripes and a single star, was fluttering
on the barricades. Catalunya Liure! (Free Cataluña) was heard on the
loudspeaker.

When evening came she went down to the little drawing room.
She was bored and wanted to smoke a cigarette. Raul, the landlady and
two guests were having coffee and listening to the radio.

"It's an uprising in Asturias," Raul said.

"Good, give me a cigarette."

Raul held his cigarette case out to her, his eyes distracted. With
a gesture of his hand he indicated that she should return to her room.
She stretched out on the bed, hearing the cries on the street, the
running along the street, the songs. *The things that happen just outside
myself,* she said to herself. A cold breeze came in from the balcony.
She got up and went to close it. *So I have to close everything that is
bothersome.* But that night she didn't manage to sleep until the very
early morning had come.

She woke up at around seven in the morning. She saw the light
under the window and heard voices again. She slipped on her bathrobe
and went to the small drawing room. They all appeared very upset.

"Is it possible to get some sleep around here?" she moaned. Raul
put his arm around her.

"Go, lie down," he said. "You know, a state of war has been

declared. The uprising has failed."

"What uprising?"

Raul's eyes contemplated her, astonished. He seized her by the chin so roughly that she had to suffocate a scream.

"It is possible?" he said. "Are you of flesh and blood or have I made you up?"

Some explosions were heard, distant, spaced out. Raul set her free and she returned to bed.

When it was already morning the Guardia Civil appeared at the far end of the street next to the Paseo de Gracia. She looked through the balcony, the barricade appeared abandoned. She went in once again. Something shook her, a thousand questions sought to move her consciousness. She sat on the edge of the bed. Suddenly Raul came in.

"Those nuts!" he exclaimed.

"What nuts?"

"They're mad."

He closed the balcony. He sat down next to her. His hands were trembling.

"What's wrong with you?"

"I don't like useless gestures," he said. "I hate useless gestures."

He lit a cigarette and his fingers were unable to control the trembling.

"A group of insane men, with a girl; they have occupied the barricade."

"I want to see them."

She was no longer able to control herself. Before he could stop her, she ran to the balcony and opened it. Down below there were about twenty men moving around. They looked like workers...and a woman. *She's a young woman, almost like me.* She closed her eyes. The sight of that young girl shook her, moved her, filled her with a dizziness that she couldn't overcome. With a brutal tug, Raul pulled her inside, threw her on the bed and once again closed the balcony.

She was there, lying down, hearing the cross-fire. One hour, two, three perhaps. She trembled, grabbed the edge of the mattress and said to herself, *I'll sink, I want to sink, I want to sink into the darkness. I don't know anything, I don't hear anything, I don't see anything.*

Then she heard the silence of the street, a marvelous, cruel silence. She could not stand up to it. Raul was not there. She felt that she was alone in the house, like she'd never have company again. It was a sensation of a horrible, despairing loneliness. She didn't dare cross the door, because she wouldn't find that silence and that loneliness. She went to the balcony, like a sleepwalker, and opened it. A pale sun illuminated the street. There were scattered clothes, weapons and papers carried away by the wind. And down below there, between the piled up paving stones, were the bodies. The stretched out body of that young girl. A road of blood advanced from somewhere, from some invisible, viscous place.

She pulled back, trembling. She threw herself stomach-first on the bed. She felt the cold of her own hands on her cheeks. *Why? Why?* screamed a voice inside her.

Two days later Raul took her from there.

"You've been ill," he said, "delirious, like a child. Come on, don't be worried anymore. We're going somewhere else. We'll never return to this part of town again."

"Why?" she said timidly. "Why have they done this? Why have they fought?"

Raul pointed at his head and his heart with a finger.

"For this reason and for this reason," he said. "Two things that you lack."

"Later, when they were already settled in the Ramblas boarding house, she saw newspapers and photographs of that event. Generally she didn't want to read newspapers. They produced an uneasy discomfort or a great loathing in her. They called the girl Rosa Libertaria de Gracia. Raul took the newspapers out of her hand.

"Drop it," he said. "These things are not for you."

Then he pointed out the Ramblas through the window pane."

"This is my thing," he said. "This is my part of town. You'll see everything is beginning now, for the two of us.)

"I never did get to tell you how I met Jeza."

"No."

"I couldn't say that my life with Raul was hell. But that's not true. That's to say I don't know if hell is all that. But I didn't suffer, I wasn't able to make out certain things, the idea of good, evil, of what is just and what is unjust... what do I know? Yes, I believe I was almost happy when I met Jeza. But that's even more strange."

The brightness of the flames blinked in Manuel's eyes.

"Do you know something, Marta? Everyone talks about Jeza. All of us, I mean…. José Taronji, Es Mariné, you, me. But when did he speak of himself? In reality what do we know of him?"

"Nobody exists more than he does."

Her voice seemed to rise from a lethargy. He covered his face with his hands, touched his closed eyelids, as though he were looking for the sockets of his eyes.

"This is what I would dare call mysterious… at the beginning we had some difficulties. But Raul immediately got ahead again and made an absurd living, if you will, but one which I liked. At least it sufficed me. Although I had to become numb in order to go on."

(They lived for a while in a big, dirty boarding house on the Ramblas. She liked to open the shutter and see the sun between the birds and the branches of the trees.

Around two in the afternoon she would wake up with a heavy head. Her eyes would hurt, she'd go to get a drink of water. A great thirst almost always filled her upon coming out of sleep. Raul would not be there anymore. Even though she'd go to bed late she knew how to wake up early if she needed to. She had strange qualities. Knowing how to bite her tongue, her self-esteem, pride, dignity and doing whatever she had to for her advantage.

"Girl, this is the way the world is. The big fish eats up the little one. Everything is fair to avoid being eaten up. Don't you agree?"

"I agree," she said as she yawned.

"Didn't you want to live?"

She didn't know whether that was life, but she liked it.

"Dionisia cleared the way for me. But don't worry. We'll come out of it ahead. This is the way I began before I met her. You'll see, you and me alone now."

They were eating in a cheap restaurant, and the unfolded newspaper was spread out in front of his face. *That's why he always buys big newspapers, to hide behind them when he talks*, she thought.

During the first month they went from here to there. From the boarding house on the Ramblas they passed to another one, more modest, on the Conde del Asalto street. Raul began to make contact with his former friends. At night, from seven or eight on, they began to drink. She began to acquire a taste for drinking.

"You can help me," Raul would say. "You're pretty although

you're not very clever. A handsome woman can be very effective."

"All right."

"But don't take initiatives, because you're not intelligent. Always pay attention to me. If you let yourself be guided by me, everything will be all right."

"As you wish."

Drinking was pleasant because everything acquired a distinct dimension…the world, human beings, the city. The city was very different after a few drinks. The people became more amusing, nicer, more surprising. At night she frequented Raul's place of action. Small and obscure cabarets of the quarter where florists, concierges, doormen and former friends of Raul spread out their nets. Raul carried money with him when he made deals with Elena and Dionisia.

"With this and my knowledge, it's only the beginning."

In the same Plaza del Teatro he set up the information bureau a little later. It was a big, dusty apartment with very high doors painted white, with polished window panes. The two rooms that looked out on the street acted as an information bureau; and the rooms behind those, as living quarters. Raul bought new furniture, carpeted the floor in red, and hung curtains on the doors and windows. Opaque and depressing rooms contrasted with the cold and oppressive Out Patient Clinic. Raul liked the overdone styles that reminded him of his "General Headquarters" (as he called the Excelsior, the Eden Concert). The Clinic was near a whorehouse. The girls were in the habit of coming around eleven in the morning, and from three to five in the afternoon. At night it remained open, and a huge parade of customers would filter through until very early in the morning. Like the Hotel before, the Clinic was the cover-up for resuming the cocaine and morphine traffic.

"You see, Marta, everything is arranged," said Raul on the day they settled into their new living quarters. The male nurse, Antonito, was a middle-aged man with thick curls of suspicious black and with deep, sad eyes. He had known Raul for some time.

"Since the very first, *Don* Raul has been very good to me. He always had a heart of gold for me."

At times a girl would run up to make a little angel, as Antonito said. Raul painted the Panhard a light blue.

"But I'm going to exchange it for a Voisin," he said. "It's

faster.")

"Almost since the first day I saw him something drew me to him in an irrevocable way. He was like an irresistible force. I used to say to myself, *life that I desire so much and love so much, that I have sought so desperately, is now here.*"

(In the same way as I am now faced with my own death. Few people can contemplate coldly, with serenity, their own death, as we two. But someone will find out some day; perhaps my own son will ask for the reason and, perhaps, it might not be useless.)

"Everything about Jeza was this way. You know something, Manuel?" she laughed lightly, "there was no way of escaping from him. Nobody was able to understand that. Raul less than anybody, that's clear. They were made for each other. The same projects, the same illusions... Raul said on that day, 'Keep one thing in mind, Marta, Jeza will bring death to you.' I was intransigent, uneducated, almost insensitive. Something special happened with him, as if he made me see the difference, for the first time, between sun and shadow, as if he had put in relief for me all the things that, up to then, had appeared opaque. The truth was that he did nothing to attract me. It was I who followed him, through my own will. Almost against his. The truth, the sure thing, is that I'll never know if he loved me or simply accepted me."

The flames were dying down and the boy's profile was scarcely distinguishable, the boy still kneeling in front of the fireplace.

"I remember it was like an absurd repetition. First mother, on that day when she surprised Raul and me, saying, 'He'll kill you. He burns everything he touches like fire.' And then Raul saying to me, 'You're lost if you follow him. He's like death. He will bring everything to ruin, you can't do that, there is something in the two of you that doesn't tie together. It's like pretending to unite water and fire. Believe me. You're hard-headed and mad, I know you well, you'll have to be sorry...'" I wasn't able to tell him, "I am not going to be sorry for anything, because it is now, the thing that I am doing now, an act of repentance, an expiation of something that, unknowingly, I betrayed, I, or someone before me." He didn't realize that I didn't choose and that I wasn't able to do anything other than what I was doing.

("It bothered you a great deal to walk around in San Juan so poorly dressed, didn't it?"

"Yes."

"Then if you are a good girl you will have everything you want."

"They say I have very poor taste."

"That may be. You will soon learn. For the moment I have not seen you with your hair combed."

They bought a lot of dresses, cheap things, costume jewelry. Raul was generous and was proud of her beauty. She seemed to grow.

"You know what I'm telling you, it seems as if you're taller. But you should drink less. I think it's beginning to harm you."

It was impossible to give up drinking. Around seven they would have cocktails, then they'd go out to dinner. Especially when foreigners came... Raul was associated with Claude Rimole, a very well-mannered and well-dressed gentleman. He had a box reserved at the Eden. When he and Raul would exchange stories, she'd become bored and drink. Raul was very fond of champagne, and she liked it better than almost anything else. Champagne, ratty, rancid and velvet, and Havana cigars were Raul's taste. They almost always went to bed at dawn. They'd wake up at noon, their heads foggy, their eyes aching. Her clothes would be scattered on the floor. With her eyes closed, she'd look for the bell on the night-table. Martina, a fat woman, a former actress without eyebrows, who cleaned the apartment, would bring them breakfast in bed in the morning. Sometimes she'd vomit. She'd look a little pale, but pretty.

"There's nothing I can do with you," Raul said. You're the most handsome woman in the world."

But, soon, what she feared, was a certainty.

"Raul, I'm going to have a baby."

"You're joking."

At the beginning he didn't believe her. Then, he had to be convinced.

"That's all right, don't worry, it's nothing, don't be worried, it's nothing, don't be afraid. Trust me."

She didn't have time to recall, nor to think. A terror that was born from the void grew in her.

"Soon, Raul, let it be very soon," she said. "I can't stand it."

Everything happened like a dream...the high white doors, the polished crystal. *This dirty white, this white of a child's burial. I have*

seen coaches with this dirty and sinister white. I hate the color white,
was the last thing she thought. Antonito brought her near the mask of
ether. Then the globes started spinning, and the rapid succession of
silence, of the great void, created a noisy confusion of frightful silence
in her and outside her.
    When she opened her eyes the pain burned, it was a living moan.
She turned her head and there it was, the horrible bucket with bloody
remains. She bit back a scream that was not born in her throat but came
from a very remote zone, behind her, to him, to all that she could
remember or foretell, a scream like a jump backward in the immense
void.
    "Don't cry," said Raul. "Everything has gone very well."
    "I'm not crying." And she felt a mute and violent wrath against
him, *to think that I'm crying, the stupid jerk, to think that I'm crying*.)
    "I met Jeza in June of 1935. I remember being ill for a few days.
I was worn out, I drank a lot. I almost didn't eat. I had remained very
thin and Raul said, 'We ought to go to the beach for a few days, or to
some other place. The truth is that we never see the sun.' It was true.
Suddenly, I realized that, when the sun shone, we were never awake.
We were like otters and rats, always in the dark. I thought I didn't even
know the color of my own skin under the sun. It seemed as though the
sun were a lion, like some idol. I had read somewhere that, in
antiquity, the sun was a ferocious idol to whom they had to throw live
girls in order to feed him. Or Dionisia had told me that. The case is that
the sun appeared to be our veritable enemy. And as spring was
beginning, we went to spend a few days in a small town on the coast.
When we returned home, Jeza had phoned. I had never seen him. He
had just arrived at the city.
    (Jeza left his telephone number. Martina noted it down, with
numbers like insects running over the paper. Raul remained very
serious.
    "When did he call?"
    "Yesterday, the day before yesterday. Today, too."
    Raul walked up and down for a while, like when something
bothered him. The paper, with the telephone number, trembled in his
hand. He rolled it up, then unrolled it.
    "Something bad?" she asked.
    "No."

Finally he phoned, spoke briefly.

Then he told her, "I don't know when I'll be back tonight, don't wait up for me."

He went out. She felt tired, a vague melancholy filled her. She had just spent a week in the sun, only in the sun. Stretched out on the sand, with her eyes closed, she had not drunk, she slept at night. Her skin had a tanned color. Something like a rare mixture of sadness and sweetness was born in her. *Something is happening to me, as though I were ending something, and as though I were on the edge of something else that I don't even know.*

She was in bed when Raul came back. She didn't go out, not even for dinner. A faint but persistent fatigue kept her from sleeping. She breathed softly, looking at the darkness. She heard the key and the crack in the door lit up. She heard footsteps, Raul's and someone else's. Two voices joined together. The light went on in the room next door. She heard people talking in a low voice. Raul's steps drew near. He entered the room and she heard him ask softly, "Are you asleep?"

"No, I'm awake."

Raul came close and turned on the lamp on the bedside table. The pink lamp shade scattered a pasty light. Raul sat on the edge of the bed. There was something in his look, a fire that she had never seen before.

"He's mad," he said bluntly.

His eyes were swollen. She listened to him with a new curiosity like an unusual thirst to learn something, to know something about him, of whomever.

"Why has he come?"

"Ah, his ideals," he laughed. "He has to be stupid. He doesn't realize that here the Party has little to do. He's been totally overtaken by the Worker Peasant Block, the CNT and the FAI. The Trotskyites, the anarchists, have leaders, they have started a true revolutionary campaign to support all the movements of the working class…last year, during the October events, do you remember? They refused to participate. They said that the proletarian class had no interest in this uprising."

Terrified, she contemplated the trembling of Raul's lips. She wasn't sure if she understood him. But it was obvious that she stumbled over his words, as when she bent halfway over, anxiously with her braid hanging down, toward the Casa de los Negros. *I want to live*. Then a voice emerged which said, *I want to know why these two men move each other by something more than surviving, by something more than living this way*. She felt weak, something was giving way in her; a sensation like fear opened a way through the fog in which it was so pleasant to get wrapped up.

"How do you know all these things?" she asked. You had never spoken to me this way."

Suddenly there was something violent, almost savage, in Raul's look.

"What do you think? That I've always been a bastard?"

"I don't know if you are." She tried to smile, the way he liked her to. When he answered, he said, "I like you because you don't have a brain, or a heart, or a conscience."

"In any case it doesn't appear serious to me," she remarked.

"Do you believe that it was always like this? No. Before this I was like him. One day I showed you where we were born and grew up together, where we had so many plans, so much hope...."

The word fell heavily. *So much hope*, he thought. *And me, hope for what, for what, toward what?* He was growing old, getting sick, dying. He could feel a sharp and ferocious sadness, an immense void, splitting him in half. It was happening to him. A painful sadness that had nothing to do with what threatened him once, in a sordid room of the Fuenterrabia hotel.

"Nothing can be done." Raul got up, helped himself to a drink, and with it in his hand, returned to the edge of the bed. "Nothing. I've already told him so. 'Look, drop all this. There's no place for you here.'"

"What does he want to do?"

He shrugged his shoulders impatiently.

"His own thing. To attract, to search out, people who can be useful in case of an uprising. Don't let him count on me. All that was over with some time ago. I have received too many blows, life is too short to waste it on utopias. I have already told him so. Don't count on me.

"Has he asked you for something?"

"Not specifically. He never asks for anything. He just talks. At one time he poisoned me that way. Not now."

"Now he thought he could count on you?"

"Perhaps…"

He remained silent, with his mouth open, his eyes suddenly harsh. The light drew out a cruel, almost harmful brightness from the edge of his glass. He turned off the light and threw himself, fully dressed, beside her. She felt his hand caressing her arm. She heard his breathing and, suddenly, he appeared to her to be a stranger. More than that. She realized that he was a stranger, that nothing united them, that everything between the two of them had ended. The great void was becoming more and more wide.

"Why unveil things that have happened, what's the purpose? Damn it, why come here, tearing up memories? Let him go away, let him leave. He is defilement," he laughed with a rough voice. "Defilement for a man like him. Why sniff in the garbage? Let him leave. I don't remember anything anymore, I am no longer the little, docile, Raul, poisoned by his integrity. Away with all that!" An old pain was reborn in him. "Everything now remains very old, very far off for me." His voice almost trembled when he added, 'The world is going to change.' To change! Yes, it was going to change because two poor boys believed it. To change hunger, injustice."

"Why hunger?" she said timidly.

But he must not have heard it, and he continued.

"Because two boys were dreaming. Two poor, ridiculous boys, studying obstinately at night, working like mules in the cleaning supplies store of magnanimous uncle Pablo who had compassion on the orphans of his poor, stupid brother, letting them work like pack animals during the day in an evil smelling and cold shop, letting them sleep in a garret under the roof in exchange for a filthy dish of potatoes, for shoes with holes in the soles… Ah, Marta… what can you know of hunger and poverty. We studied at night because he decided to. He always planned everything, outlined it, with his accursed and venomous words. 'It's going to change the world, Raul. Raul, it's not necessary to change life, it is necessary to change the world'… Life passes quickly, children grow up. Poor Jeza. Mad. He's mad."

There was a feeling of crying some place, that no one could perceive.

He used to buy books, with his miserly pay. We were intelligent, Marta, even uncle Pablo used to say, "Too intelligent for me. I don't forbid you to study if you work during the day like good boys. But the light bulb must not be turned on after ten o'clock at night." We used to buy candles, we took turns working. On the night before exams, what insomnia, what obstinacy, what willpower. When they gave me the scholarship we thought that the world was beginning. Uncle said, "I'll have to start believing in you"... But, on the following day, back to work. Go downstairs, the black shop. The dream like a nightmare, like a ghost. At times I couldn't take it. I would fall. He gave me a shove with his elbow, unaffected, as though I didn't have nerves, blood or soul. One day he took me to the courtyard and put my head under the water trough. 'Our time will come soon,' he said. 'Hold on.' Our time! Mine, yes, arrived. He was already a lawyer. I finished the course of studies and then what? Our uncle died and his widow didn't want to see us—he imitated the whining voice of a woman. 'He did enough for you. He permitted you to study for a profession and he helped you.' Very well. A professional course of studies, Raul Zarco, doctor. And then? Bury oneself in a miserable town, let life pass by, the world that was going to change...? He was made of different stuff. Not me. I am a man. I want to live. To live. Life soon passes by, Marta. He was no longer at my side, poisoning me, poisoning us.... He's not a man, he's a fever. A devouring fever, like the plague."

She heard this troubled breathing next to the tick-tock of the clock. Suddenly he became angry.

"And everything, for what purpose? For what purpose? Right now he doesn't have many options. I have told him so. 'Moscow doesn't pay attention, is not interested in us, they are experiencing their own problems in Moscow.' The split has left an impression on our minds, the Party is in a dormant situation, it doesn't act. The split doesn't favor him."

"What is he going to do?"

Everything is confused, he doesn't quite understand; but something is opening up, a way in the fog.

"Officially, study Catalan statute law. It will be important only among university people. The working classes consider it anti-revolutionary. With what happened last October and the repression that followed, the working class sees itself harassed, through the fault of an ill-prepared uprising."

She remembered the barricade in the Calle Mayor de Gracia street and Rosa Libertaria. She felt the cold, raised the sheet up to her chin and closed her eyes.

"Be quiet," she said. "Tomorrow you will tell me everything."

Raul began to take off his clothes.

"Forget all this. These things must not worry you. For the moment you'll have to bear with it for a couple of days with us. But I suppose that he'll find a house that suits him far away from here."

"Is he going to live with us?"

"I have asked him to," he had fear in his voice, almost. *Of himself, perhaps.* "I have asked him to, I've said to him, 'Stay here for a few days until you find something better. Stay with us for a little while, I beg you.'"

He turned around with a rapid movement. And he said a strange thing,

"I love him, Marta. Although I don't like him, I can't help but love him."

"Who is he?"

"Didn't I tell you? He's my brother.")

"But I didn't see him until two days later, almost by chance."

(Jeza appeared, taking her by surprise. He was there, beside her.

"I can't be with you, I'm sorry," Raul was saying." Understand me, life changes, life takes bearings in another direction. Now it is too late to go back. I'm sorry, Jeza, you know that I appreciate you, you know that I truly love you. But that's the way things are."

Then Jeza appeared in the light and, for the first time, she saw his face. His eyes, brilliant and blue, showed something cold and angry at the same time.

He looked at her from top to bottom. She felt a vague, fragile unease, like the small flame that arose between Jeza and herself, while Raul lit a cigarette.

"Don't you know her?" Raul said, bantering. "She's my little daughter."

Jeza kept on looking at her, without saying anything. Raul put his hand on her head.

"You've grown up, haven't you?"

She felt a blow inside, and began to laugh with her eyelids half-closed so that no one could see her eyes. A strange feeling of a growing echo in the void was opening up, like the waves when someone throws a rock into the quiet water. It seemed that they were in a highly domed place, where her voice resounded, where the echo of something was in the air, not a voice but, perhaps, a rare coming together of things, not of persons but of objects. She opened her eyes once more and Jeza kept looking at her. A lock of his hair, almost white, fell over his right eyebrow. A smooth, soft hair and, nevertheless, rebellious.

"Well, tell him the truth," said Raul, his big teeth near to her, "tell him that you love me a great deal."

"I don't feel like laughing."

"What's wrong with you?" He grabbed her chin. And then she realized: so many, many times he had seized her this way, harshly, raising her to him and saying, *this is good, this is bad. How many things he taught her. You don't have to learn anything. You're all right the way you are. I like you that way.* The only important thing in the world was to please him, to appear right to him. *When I am old they'll make fire wood out of me, like Stromboli would chop up poor Pinocchio.*

Jeza left without saying good-bye.

"He's rude." Raul drained his glass. "Don't pay attention to it. It's not his fault. No one taught him to be any other way."

"But you are his brother," she said timidly.

"Yes, that's the difference. They didn't teach me anything either. I learned everything by myself, you know. Just like you."

A pink residue remained at the bottom of his glass, a strange lost ruby.

"The same plans, the same desires…. Bah! for what purpose? Life is short and sad. You have to exhaust it. And life will have thrown him over, like a wolf."

"And not you?"

"Me, too," he said laughing. But before that, I will have gotten a good lucrative post. Don't believe it, but I also had my doubts. It was always the same. I never saw anyone more consistent. While life has taught me to change, to shift, it has not been of any use to him. And there's no doubt he bears its scars. But he doesn't understand, he doesn't learn…"

At that moment Raul seemed surprised. There was a nervous trembling in his fingers.

"Shall we go?"

He took her by the arm and they went out. The night was coming on softly.

"Don't you have any regrets?" she said laughing.

An unusual, whitish powder covered the sidewalk like a patina.

"I don't like this place," she said suddenly full of anguish. "I don't like anything. Let's get away from here, please. Any place, wherever."

"Why? Don't be stupid. Now you're going home, get dolled up and we'll go some place around there. You'll soon see how you will change your opinion. There is no place in the world better than this."

"I don't feel like it."

She was in a bad mood. And the worst thing was that she didn't feel like staying or going away. For the first time she began to understand her mother's changes of mood. *This is tedium,* she thought. *Or, perhaps the beginning of wisdom.* She yawned and felt like laughing.

"You don't have a heart," Raul said. "What I like best about you is that you don't have a heart."

She never understood what he was saying to her…. She kissed him and let herself be led gently.

On the following day Martina brought her breakfast. She made strange gestures with her eyes and mouth.

"What's wrong with you?"

"Ah, don't you know? It's horrible. The butcher's daughter, that girl with the face of an angel…do you remember her?"

"What do I know? I'm not acquainted with anyone around here."

"Well, she's seventeen…. You see now, she had a child three or four days ago without anyone knowing anything about it. Nobody, not even her father or her brothers discovered it. Well, it appeared this morning, quartered, and in the garbage can. A man passes by every morning with a little cart, and takes away the grease, the bones, things like that. There was the baby, in pieces, like a chicken…"

"Shut up, shut up!…," she screamed. A great trembling filled her. She covered her ears. But the scream, that great ancient scream floated toward her, again, from some obscure place. "Take this away, I'm not hungry."

"Ah, yes, of course." Martina's laugh was bitter, cruel. She picked up the tray. But she turned her head and spit.

"You don't want to know that. You don't want to know anything, do you? Well, my girl, there is a bit of everything in life. Everything. A bit of everything. Not just sprees and drunken bouts in life."

She covered her head with the sheet, closed her eyes with force. She didn't get up until seven in the evening. She was silent.

"You're acting oddly," said Raul. "Are you feeling sick?"

"No. It's just that I want to be alone."

5

Spring was seething under the cement that covered the earth, the stones, the well-arranged and confined lawn of the flower beds, the saddened trunks of the trees. A muzzled flash of lightning was moving about and threatened to break out and tremble. Something pushed the earth from inside out and the trees, in the first breath of dawn, were flooded with a resplendent confusion.

She had no more news of him other than the crack of light under his door at night. The light murmur of his steps going up or down the stairs, the hidden muteness which kept her tense, impelled her more and more toward him. The stupid words, Raul's disquiet, her own emptiness. It was that night when Claude Rimole came again, when she said, "I'm not going with you. I want to remain alone. I feel like being alone. I have already told you so."

Raul looked at her without any expression.

"Perhaps it would suit you to return to the beach for a few days." The Clinic smelled horrible. The light shimmered on the polished window panes.

"Let's get away from here, Raul. I want to go and live some place else."

Raul did not answer. He was looking in the mirror with his back to her. His black hair was shining on the back of his neck. He was looking at himself attentively, scrutinizing himself.

"I'll be back late."

Jeza's room opened facing her bedroom.

First she knocked with her knuckles but nobody answered. She opened the door and saw him, as she would see him so many times afterward, her whole life. He was seated in front of his papers, in shirt-sleeves and holding a black pencil. The little glass light fixture cast a soft light over his head. The lock of hair was on his forehead, soft and rebellious, shining prematurely white. He was only two years older than Raul. His eyes were a transparent blue, cold and fixed; they contemplated her.

"Are you leaving?" she asked.

She had just seen the suitcase, with its buckled straps, swollen and pot-bellied, waiting, like a dog, against the wall. "Yes."

He scarcely moved his lips, he said it more with a movement of his head. She did not know shyness, but, in that moment, she felt almost mute, her hands trembled, and a strange coldness gradually overwhelmed her.

"Where? Aren't you all right here?"

He said something, but she couldn't hear him. She vaguely understood a brief explanation. His glance, fixed and quiet, dispassionate, on her. She sat down on the stool, next to him, in spite of noticing his impatience. His eyebrows that were highly raised, the questioning glance.)

"On the night that he was leaving our house I went to see him, I said to him, 'Why are you leaving? Aren't you happy with us?' I don't know what he answered, I scarcely remember. But I remained there, I couldn't separate myself from him. Something controlled me, something that still has not left me," Marta said.

(Jeza was rather tall and, by the color of his skin and his eyes, it could be said that he was blond.

"What's wrong with you?" he said.

Suddenly, that question wiped all words away. She said to herself, *that's right, what's wrong with me?*

"I don't know," she murmured.

He said so few useless things, he spoke so little; in spite of what Raul said, "He does nothing but talk, he doesn't ask for anything, talking is what is typical of him." And she thought, *It isn't that he doesn't talk, it's that he doesn't waste his time or his words.*

"No, it's not an illness. I'm restless. I'd like to go someplace that isn't the Eden Concert or the Excelsior... someplace where they don't drink that horrible champagne that Raul likes so much, or always talk about the same things."

She raised her hand to her forehead and noticed that something was moistening her palms.

"Fine," she tried to smile. "Perhaps the only thing that's happening is that I'm tired."

"Don't you want to go to bed and sleep?"

His voice surprised her. In his voice there wasn't dryness nor even interest. While saying so, he rubbed the space between his eyebrows with his index finger. A gesture that, later, would become so familiar to her. He left the pencil on the table. His glance was the only thing that could be seized.

"No, I can't sleep. Don't you want to go and take a walk with me?"

"Now? Isn't it late?"

"No. Late for what?"

Only then did he smile. He got up, went to get his jacket hanging from the back of the chair and threw it over one shoulder, like a peasant. He looked at her, as though waiting for something.

He raised his hand to his neck to adjust his tie that was hanging loose. And then she felt taken by that hand, tied to that hand. Something pressed her throat, a question, a stupid question opened its way between her and the world. *What am I doing, why am I living, what's happening around me, and in me? Why do I love no one?*

"Do you want to walk?" he asked.

"Yes, fine, let's walk. Take a long walk."

He walked beside her, without looking at her, but she felt him very near. She accommodated her steps to his and took his arm. He bent his elbow slightly. He was not stiff, but there was no softness in him. Under the gentle pressure of his fingers, she noted that he could have a frightening hardness.

She stopped, without daring to turn her head or look at him.

"What's the matter with you?"

She did not answer. She was surprised. For a moment she was eager to draw back, to go back and hide herself, to sink and be stupefied in Raul's world of red velvet, with its perfume of violets and alcohol; the bedroom, the foggy parlor of the Excelsior, the theatre box of the Eden Concert, where the world sank in a curtain of seaweed and smoke. Forgetfulness, unconsciousness; she no longer felt curiosity. The void was waiting once more, *I know now what is awaiting me, I am foretelling it, I'm going to know something that perhaps I don't want to know,* screamed the voice that, for some time, had opened a path in her, that ran over the walls of her consciousness, like a lost chill in a dark, abandoned house.

"Do you want to go back home?"

It surprised her not to notice even impatience in his tone. *I went with him to importune him, I scarcely know him. I have no right, only because I'm his brother's friend, to interfere with his time.* He was waiting for her, not with patience or affection, not even with kindness. *I'm sure that he doesn't know what kindness is, Antonito would never say that he has a heart of gold, perhaps he would say that he doesn't even have a heart, all of him is too real, too certain in this fog, he seems like a tree, he can act as a guide or one can dash against him, it's something like a wall, or that flat and terrible sea that at times frightens and can't be looked at.*

"No, I don't want to return. You know, I've been drinking too much lately," she tried to give a joking tone to her voice.

But he looked at her without smiling. He held back his words, simply. *He doesn't even feel curiosity, it's as though he didn't have blood.* And, nevertheless, there was the curve of his lips, warm and human. His arm, alive, under her fingers.

"If it doesn't bother you," he said precipitously, as though wanting to remove whatever was opening a path, like a wind, "we could go toward the sea."

"Toward the sea? Very well."

She said it softly, almost with sweetness. He then slipped his hand beneath her arm, drew her towards him, and she noticed her side clinging to his, and a rare notion of equilibrium between their two bodies. *Nothing angular, nor heavy*, she said to herself, *that's the word. It results in something comfortable.* The idea amused her, she turned to look at him. But he continued silent, distant. He was walking beside her. He simply walked beside her.

They left the Ramblas behind. The trees ended there, where the birds screamed in the early morning hours.

"If you're getting tired we can catch a taxi."

"No, I prefer to walk."

To go, to walk and not stop is perhaps the only thing I want. Then he asked her an unexpected question.

"What is your name?"

He doesn't remember it. Raul had told it to him and he doesn't even remember it. She had to repeat it twice. They didn't speak any more, she had to repeat it twice. They didn't talk any more, she didn't remember hearing him say anything more until they arrived there. Until he was suddenly there, in such a strange, somnambulate way. *Because we advance awkwardly through a river which has banks of faces, of thoughts, banks of men and women and children, chairs seen so many times. The chairs of the street await on both sides the main road, like those trains of lies made up by children.* They were dusty chairs, some advertising an aperitif, or something else, nice and useless. When the sun shone perhaps they sheltered childrens' whisperings, or old peoples' wandering or sedentary glances, perhaps some modestly held sadness. Nothing indicated whether in daylight or in the late afternoon shade that the hidden beat of fear, despair or simple helplessness could take refuge there. The wandering shadows of the birds passed each other, the shadow of the branches fell, the green swaying of the leaves impelled by the wind. The heat and the dust would rise from the asphalt within a month, perhaps two, and the noise of the street would suffocate, kill whatever hidden pain, or, simply, whatever emptiness that was like the one she felt. *There are only bodies of men and women,* she tried to reason, anguished, drowned in her great emptiness, *limited number of bodies or superfluous bodies, that look at other men, other women, passing by, that are resting....* But they were late at night; and in the early hours when she was struggling, everything was changing, and she scarcely held everything. *Old people and young people, vagabonds, solitary beings. Rest, melancholy, fear, hunger,* she thought. *Tranquil or sorrowful refuge.* The edges of the streets gradually took on limits, bodies were showing up as though thrown out on its two banks at night. Just the way the remains of shipwrecked boats, dead seaweed, sea stars that had lost their brilliance, mysterious empty shells would appear on the sand. *One never knows when the first one will appear,* she said to herself, little by little, like the cold stars of a winter sky. The bodies seldom became transparent. *They are no longer bodies that hide and keep things like closed boxes. In the silence, when all words and smiling lies have fled, just like the birds, one has a dream populated by high branches where, finally, one can hide oneself, wander through my emptiness, failure, hope, perhaps that which was a call to the heart. It's like an opening and shutting of butterflies that tremble in the night, faced with indifference; a man sleeping, with his body half bent, his shoulder blades standing out under the thin jacket, like the withers of an old, defeated horse; prudent sleep, put on its guard by an old man in a shirt with very short sleeves, the back of his neck grey, vanquished like an anticipation of death that is drawing near; the woman thrown headlong, with her empty hands on her lap; the vigilant, solitary man sunk in a sleep more distant, with his eyes open, sheltered as I am now, in some remote country of the memory, present and absent, always distant.* She kept on walking, without knowing whether she had fallen asleep or awakened. In the center of the main road life and night flowed; and, on the shores—just like those plants on the edges of the river, which, when she was a girl, she imagined to be poisonous—emerged sad and dark silhouettes, gestures of a certain and pathetic world, *indifference, hope, lameness.* As though against the light of her shoulders, of immobile torsos, of heads, she thought she saw a variegated altar-piece, cabalistic or diaphanous. Fatigue, loneliness, struggle or abandonment. The springing from life, like a fountain, a confined artery, rebellious, that wanted to leap out, broken, through the skin of the world. *Perhaps it is not silence that is inside me, but a grandiose clamor that I don't even perceive,* she said to herself with a shudder.

She pressed against his arm, like a shipwreck, and her own fear made her say, "I don't like living."

She said it without realizing it. They were already next to the beach. *As on that night, on that other occasion, in San Juan with Raul, I also went to the beach. And how different everything was. Then I also had on sandals*—now she had on women's shoes with high, uncomfortable, absurd red heels—*full of sand.* She bent over, she felt an ill-defined heaviness, something like the dark and inexplicable shame of some undefined guilt. She took off her shoes, staggered. He held her by the arm more forcefully.

She dropped to her knees, feeling the greasy, dirty dampness of the sand. A slight wind moved her hair and she closed her eyes. The smell of the beach emerged from the ground, she felt it in the air. The wind was sticky under her skin. She opened her eyelids and saw that the night was disappearing. The day was not coming on, but the night was turning pale gold; a whiteness, diaphanous and terrible, was arriving, more guessed at than real, an infinity of small bits of glass shone in the sand. *This whiteness is known to me,* frightens me, it is the whiteness of the dead. Like a flock of uncertain animals that advances and retreats, the sea moaned, without daring at all to strike, *threatening, threatening, with some terrible prophecy. Like the muffled lament of the world in which I live, to which I have turned my back.* The silhouettes of the boats were delineated in the light. He was beside her, also kneeling in the sand, looking at her.

"I don't like living," she repeated.

"But," he said without irritation and without consternation. "How can you like or not like it, if you don't know what it is."

For the second time she saw him smile. His smile was surprising, almost childlike.

"Try to think a little about the life of others. Perhaps that would help."

"If I want," she said in a very low voice. "I am not intelligent, everyone has always told me I'm not useful for very much. But I have never felt pain until now."

He held out his hand to her, for the first time. She, with a sudden gesture, took it in hers.

The profiles and silhouettes around them became clear. The concession stand closed, its panes covered with wood boards. Light was pouring down from the sky like a liquid over a smooth surface.

From the darkness behind her emerged the dirty facades, the rubbish, the brighter stains of clothing being hung up to dry. Across the way she could see the mass of the coast, like a sleeping monster, with its lights off. In the sky thick clouds were fleeing.

A man, bent over in a curve, was walking here and there, chasing papers pushed by the wind. He had a hook in his hand and caught the paper as though it were a fish and put it in a sack. He went away, up the beach. He disappeared in the mist.

They heard the light touch of footsteps. A nocturnal animal, a child, boy or girl, one could not make it out, with a basket full of glasses and a black bottle, offered them drinks.)

"I was never able to leave him."

(Where will you go?"

"I found a little house on the Pedralbes Road."

I don't know anything about him, nor if he has a wife or children that can complicate his life, apart from his strange ideas, as Raul says. Scarcely that much Raul has told me about when they were both boys.

He kept on being a boy, the same as then. Not like all the others who, on growing up, lost track of themselves, definitely and without themselves, as sad little dwarfs, at the end of a remote road. No, he was still the same. *Thus he goes, like an arrow, to death,* she thought, with a frightening presentiment. What I feel is love, but love is not the most important thing between him and me.

When they entered the apartment everything was silent. The

Clinic closed, the whitish light, like the splendor of rain, reverberated on the polished window panes. She hated those high, white doors, the terrible smell, poorly masked by Raul's violent cologne. She hated the white and dirty world, heavy and troubled. Raul had not arrived.

She then left the bedroom, crossed the little corridor and opened Jeza's room. She went in, closed the door softly behind her, with the conviction that she was closing hatred, emptiness and perhaps nausea, behind her. Only a great question mark existed behind her, a great thirst in front of her. Jeza looked at her in silence. She came close to him, rose on her tiptoes, enveloped him with her arms and kissed him.

When she woke up the early morning was already advanced. The bed appeared empty beside her. Jeza was no longer there. But she didn't feel fear, only a faint uneasiness. She jumped out of bed and when she turned her eyes about and contemplated the great emptiness of the room, her heart turned upside down. A small rectangle of paper, like a small sail, stood out on the table. She quickly took it. He had only written down an address. She squeezed the paper between her fingers, crushed it and put it to her face. There is no way out.

She crossed to the door. The bedroom remained closed. She entered. Raul was sleeping. The tangled head, the face against the pillow as he usually did. She went to the bathroom, turned on the faucets with an almost infantile anxiety. She took a shower. There was a strange slowness in everything...a sluggish security...something, in everything, like splendor, new, inevitable...a heavy, sure fatalism, in all things and objects, even up to the least of her gestures...in her hand that she held out, in her steps, in her breath itself.

Raul appeared in the frame of the door.

"Where have you been?"

There was no violence, nor anger or jealousy in his voice. Only a fatal sound. His hair was uncombed, taken by the dark fog of sleep. *Terribly human and sad,* she thought. She tried to go through the door, but Raul's hand held her forcefully.

"Where?" he insisted.

"With Jeza."

He let go of her as though she were on fire. Raul stepped away and his eyes seemed to awaken, almost painfully.

"That's not bad," he said and tried to smile. But it was only a tired, morose pout which curved his lips. "It wouldn't be ill-conceived to think that it was you who made him change his mind. Yes, the truth is that would please me. I'll give you a prize if you earn it. The great wall bursting open, broken, by a little ant like you! It would have never occurred to me."

Once more he tried to hold her by the arm. She gently broke loose. She went to the closet, took out the little suitcase, the same one she had carried to the beach in past days.

Perhaps there was a stupor in Raul's eyes, but she didn't look at him.

"What are you doing? Where are you going?"

"I'm leaving with him."

"With him?"

He began to laugh brusquely. He sat on the edge of the bed, rubbing his hand on his forehead. His brown skin shone. He was barefoot and, again like a blow, those bare feet were those of an unknown and terrible animal walking over the world. She felt a sudden desire to put her arms around those feet, to scream, *save me Raul, save me from this abyss toward which I am walking, retrieve me, let me be enmeshed in the world you walked on, that you trample on, you, retrieve me.* But Raul's voice restored calm.

"You're mad, Marta, With him? Do you perhaps know who he is? Don't tell me that he has asked you to!"

"Nor has he told you that he loves you, or anything like that. He never says things like that."

"No."

As she heard him on the other occasion, she repeated like a pale echo.

"He never asks for anything."

Raul stood up.

"He will destroy you. That's what he'll do with you. He will destroy you, he's not human. It is something that can't even be explained. He is is going to annihilate you, as he was about to destroy me. He is death, he will lead you to death."

His voice sounded lugubrious and he himself appeared surprised by the tone.

Suddenly he blinked rapidly and added almost paternally, "Look, Marta, I don't see you together, I don't see you together. It's like combining water and fire. I don't see you together, that's true."

But he knew all that he had to say was useless and he sat down, tired, apathetic, with his hands falling over his knees.

She had just closed her suitcase. She turned around. He wasn't looking at her.

"Good-bye, Raul," she said.

She heard the squeaking of the door behind her.

6

The creaking of the treads came up from the basement. The shadow also advanced up the wall, strangely drawn out, as though stretched by its two extremes, duplicated, triplicated. There were great, loose scales on the wall. (The whole house full of ruin and desolation.) The back wall of the building was burnt down. Judging by the blackish stains on the mosaics, they had made a fire on the floor. They had turned the shutters and some of the furniture into firewood. The house, naked the way a dead person is, was open and without eyelids, still full of everything which I don't know whether I must love or forget.)

Marta took hold of the back of the old sofa. The upholstery was stained, tattered, as though full of cuts. Even before it had sheltered Esteban it had sheltered avalanches of refugees from the south. Then, successively, it was a warehouse, a depot, offices. (And, Jeza, your shadow, your strange splendor, goes from one side to the other, crosses the frame of the door, like a scream. Even like a voice crying out for something, for something that I will never succeed in understanding. I always wanted to understand you, but I only knew how to follow you. I also cry out, but for the least things, for something simple like the solitary weeping of a child up the road.)

The shadow ascended slowly. It was a boy, only a boy who was never going to reach nineteen, who was climbing the stairs, peaceful as an old man. So many times, in the last days, she saw him come upstairs like this, with the canned goods, with the plates, smiling almost happily, saying, "Don't be afraid, there is still a lot left downstairs. We have food left over." He used to eat like a child with a good appetite and laugh and point out, with his powerful man's hand—only his hands were like a man's—the window, the sun, the bare trees in the garden. He used to say, "Today we'll have a fine day, I can tell. Or, perhaps it will rain, let's close the window, there will probably be a storm." He recovered, perhaps, the tender and untranscendent happiness of children. He went to the garden and, with the hands of a Brother Gardener, he pulled out the weeds, straightened the door which no longer fitted tightly, or restored the chair which had become unglued, while joking, "This one really looks as though it had been to war." (A child, as though recently born to death, poor boy, everything seems to be born and die in him) or when preparing the meal, he'd open the cans of food, carefully, over-anxiously, biting his tongue.

A great compassion and a great fear joined together now paralyzed her, there, coming and climbing the shadow on the wall. She looked at her own hands against the back of the sofa and they looked like two frightened and cold animals. (In order that a shadow might also exist, in this case, a body with arteries, blood, life. Life and fear are as fragile as glass; fragile and hard, violent and fragile as water, like a torrent, with the powerful white light of water falling from very high up onto the earth, toward some sea where rivers and wells and all the bitter salt of the world are mixed together; thus it rises up as does the sea.) The shadow became paralyzed and the body arose, like a tree trunk floating in the darkness of the water. (I never realized how tall he is.) In his hands the weapon had a blackened, concrete weight.

"Come," said Manuel.

She obeyed. Up to that moment it was she who had impelled the light, the arrival, the waiting. Now it was he (boys are the ones irreductible and silent, strange boys, like fever, like a fever, who say, "Resist," those who say, "come, we can't retreat now. It was not a man, it isn't a man, it's a fever.") She looked at him as though it were the first time she had ever seen him. His hair, copper-gold and curling at the back of his neck, his golden skin, his big eyes.

She followed him outside. The door banged strangely at her back (never again will I cross this threshold, nor will I hear the break of these hinges, nor will I see my shadow on the ground. The sun, a pale gold, fugitive, shone over the harmful spikes of the fence. From the fog of the main road, in the curve itself, emerged flashes, echoes. A sound, repeated, opaque, like a beat, because the earth also clamors in its silence.)

There was the hedge, the stonewall, the iron fence. She knelt. The blunderbuss in his hands held up without trembling. For five consecutive days, down there in the cellar, she had heard gunfire. Everyday, every afternoon, she saw the traces of bullets on the wall (his aim was not very good). She let herself fall beside him, lean her head on the iron railing and close her eyes.

A thin dog was running up the road. His barking was lost in the direction of the mountain slope. Suddenly he wavered, then stopped dead. Then he went back and saw him pass quickly, his ears sticking up and his tongue hanging out.

In the curve of the main road the tank stood out in the fog. The lateral figures took shape in their turn approaching the trees, figures lightly fugitive. Manuel raised the blunderbuss and supported it against the edge of the wall. The silhouettes of the soldiers became more concrete. When the nearest one clearly showed his profile, Manuel pressed the trigger.

The first bursts reached the soldier, right on. She saw him stagger, fall. The second one fled behind the nearest tree. He was limping.

The tank was now closer, so much so that its belly was like a nearby animal, almost familiar.

(A single moment of silence and I think that I hear the grass, the immoderate screams of the birds, the scraping of the lizards against the wall, the gushing of the water from the world under my knees, a single moment of silence is enough to hear that.)

Roots, a dark clot of earth sprang up in the dust. The wall crumbled away, with a piece of the fence. The hedge was smoldering in the fog. A scream, two screams, some unrecognized command resounded. The window panes broke into pieces, flew in the air. The rays of the sun gathered their resplendence.

Three soldiers advanced, still firing. Only the silence answered. They searched the hedge skillfully. But only smoke emerged. The broken window panes crackled under the soles of their boots.

The first soldier came close to the pile of rocks under the collapsed fence. He bent over.

"A man and a woman," he said to himself. "Must be crazy!"

He went back, raised his hand and gestured a call for assistance. Then, with his dirty, tired forearm, he dried the sweat from his forehead.